CARNAGE

STORIES BY

WEASEL

Sinister Stoat Press

Carnage
Weasel

ISBN-13: 978-1-948712-69-9

© 2021 Izzy Torres, AKA Weasel
https://degenerateweasel.weebly.com

Front Cover Design by James, GoOnWrite.com

Editor: Jonathan W. Thurston

Sinister Stoat Press
an imprint of Weasel Press
Lansing, MI
www.weaselpress.com

Printed in the U.S.A.

10 9 8 7 6 5 4 3 2 1

CONTENTS

For Jonny

FOREWORD
JONATHAN W. THURSTON

Carnis. The old Latin word for meat, flesh, and even steak. In English: carnivore, carnival, carnal, carnage. And in true form, Weasel's book *Carnage* delivers all these things: predators that hunt in the night, carnivals with dancing animals, encounters of the carnal kind, and the eponymous carnage that concludes each tale.

I met Weasel (my now husband) through his fiction, and it was through a dark, gritty furry novella at the time. It was, at the time, the most Beat thing I had ever read. Had lots of cigarettes, booze, prostitution, swearing, and 2am nights full of contemplation. I always hold that book dear to my heart because that Dalmatian was one of my first furry crushes, and Weasel crushed my heart with what he did to that poor dog. (Never forget; never forgive.) But the color scheme for his books have changed since that one. Where *We live for Half-Moons* was all blues, grays, blacks, and reds, *Carnage* is a cavalcade of colors, a carnival of fireworks. We're all mad here, dancing on our handpaws, our dicks and tits bouncing around to a distorted carnival track where Goofy is singing "It's a Small World" on a way-too-fast carousel, but the music is too slow, but we're all high as balls, so none of it matters...Yeah, that sentence pretty much captures this book in a nutshell. And you know what? It's still my favorite of Weasel's books so far.

Part of the reason this is easily my favorite book by Weasel is that he deals with so many real horrors here. Look past all the magic. All the flash, bang, and dazzle. And you'll see domestic violence (that Weasel has lived), hookup app danger (that I've lived), and internalized homophobia (that we've all lived). Weasel is in your face with all this, and he doesn't hold back (quite characteristic of all his fiction honestly). But even for queer horror, this is just such a transgressive collection of short stories, and it challenges the way we define queer horror. Rather than just dealing with queer as a subtext or traditional horror that happens to have queer characters, he really focuses on uniquely queer horrors and anxieties.

Per the name of the book, too, what is carnal and what is carnage blur. You will find yourself horrified. You will find yourself aroused. And hopefully, you'll find yourself uncomfortable when you feel both of those things at the same time. I know I did! It's such a tough talent, and I've rarely seen it executed well: Clive Barker, Bill Kieffer, and Amber Dawn to name a few. But again, what these authors lack is that raw edge, that Beat background, Weasel has. So yeah, if Allen Ginsberg and Clive Barker had a furry baby that came out of the womb vaping like a hipster Tex Avery cartoon and demanding a blowjob (something I could see more from the baby in Who Framed Roger Rabbit?), that'd be Weasel. And this would be his magnum opus (at least thus far).

So, I guess I get to be the bouncer for once. Can I see your ID please? Cool. Just wanted to make sure you're old enough. And can you sign this waiver please? Yep, just right here...and right there...and initial there. Oh, it's just normal liability stuff. City ordinances, you get the idea. Great. Now, yes, please leave your clothes at the door. Yeah yeah, strict dress code. Less you think about it, the better it'll be for you. And yeah, no phone service once you're inside, sorry. You're good to go now! Thank you for coming (it won't be the last time tonight), and welcome, one and all, to Carnage.

Content Warning

This book contains scenes of graphic violence, sexual violence, gore, murder, alcohol, smoking, sex, homophobia, blood, domestic violence, non consent, cannibalism, blood, suicidal ideation, body hatred, death, self-harm, kidnapping, mental & verbal abuse.

CARNAGE

PROLOGUE

Pink and blue neon enveloped Rachel's fur as she approached the haunted house. The world dead around the lioness, she stood in front of the huge sign that read "Carnage," and checked her phone. The glare illuminated the green of her eyes as she looked at the screen, the beige of her fur coming back for a moment while she remained under neon lights and darkness. She had nothing waiting for her. No missed calls, no unanswered texts, and even twitter had calmed down for the night as she waited for the haunted attraction to open. She could see her breath leave her body, as if a small puff of smoke were leaving her. Rachel walked in a small circle as she waited, cursing herself for wearing the tight jean jacket. Though it kept her warm, it was not as comfortable. *I may want to look good, but shit, why do I gotta wear the most uncomfortable shit? I ain't impressin' anybody,* she thought to herself.

The woods remained silent around her. Cracks, rustling leaves, a breeze, they all lay dormant. Rachel was in the middle of nothing. She thought that the building in front of her took haunted to another level. The stairs leading up to the door looked decrepit, the roof was sinking to the earth, and the door looked as if it had been ripped down the middle. A feeling of unease started to flow through her as she started to really examine the place and her surroundings, realizing that she was completely alone in the middle of nothing. Unsure of where the nearest store of gas station was, she checked her phone to ensure she had service and kept it ready if she needed to.

The flyer she got in the mail stated the house would open at midnight. What better way to get scared than to take a tour in a haunted house at midnight? Carnage was said to be extreme. She spent weeks watching videos on YouTube to see what she would be in for, but each experience she witnessed was different. As she stood there alone, Rachel wondered what her experience would be like, and if she would be safe inside. From the videos she witnessed, it seemed not everyone was prepared or ready for what hit them behind the walls of Carnage.

Her phone buzzed. Rachel rushed to open the text which read, "You are the queen of bad ideas!" *That motherfucker, Mike!* she thought to herself and started to text back.

"At least I got ideas! What the fuck you doing tonight? Jerkin' off?" She shot back and checked the time. She still had another fifteen minutes to kill before anything would start.

"I'm behind you. Check us out!" Her eyes quickly scanned around her. At first she didn't notice him in the darkness, but eventually the basset hound emerged into the neon, his wolf boyfriend latched to his arm. Mike smoothed his hand through the fur of his head then waived to Rachel as they approached. His brown and white splotches were washed away as the blue neon sign pulled them in. Allen found himself a purple hue as the red and grey of his fur meshed with the neon.

The wolf kissed Mike on the cheek, then scanned the area

around them. His gold eyes fixated on every detail he could see. Rachel looked him over. She stared at how bright his fur was under the neon, even though when taken out he would be a normal red and gray boy. "So, when's this thing supposed to start? Looks creepy as shit already," he said while lighting a cigarette.

Mike looked over at Rachel. He thought back to all the times she had said she was going into Carnage. He almost didn't want to come that night, but curiosity got the better of him. "Figured you might want some company, Rach," the hound said. "Plus, if the timing's right, I could take wolf boy here for a fuck in a secluded spot." He fidgeted with his coat, trying to close it over his small belly. Allen put a hand on the hound and kissed his cheek.

Rachel scanned the two, a little annoyed but relieved she wasn't going to go through the experience alone. "You always gotta find some place to fuck, don't you?" she said teasingly.

"I mean, duh! You can't not fuck in a haunted house, Rachel. It's like fucking in a graveyard, you need to do it once for clout," said Allen as he continued smoking his cigarette.

"I'd be more sheepish about it, but he's right," Mike said, shrugging. Rachel always thought Bassett hounds were weird, their flesh bulging up with different expressions. She thought to herself that she wouldn't want that burden. *I got enough of my own shit to think about without the worry of fat shaming myself more than I do already.*

"At least you honest," she responded briefly. "But you paying for yourselves. The doors are about to open."

Mike raised his hands. "No worries; I got us all." Before the hound could say anything further, the door opened, and a large goat emerged. His fur a blend of black, yellow and red, he walked down the broken steps. His horns stretched out far from his head. His body carried two massive golden towers reaching towards the empty sky above the group.

3

"Welcome, welcome everyone!" His voice was booming; a gruff low tone emitting from his throat as he thrust his hands open.

This motherfucker looks like he from a Willy Wonka rip-off, Rachel thought to herself as she studied the purple suit he wore. She was thankful he didn't have a cane.

His eyes looked over the small group before him. The goat adjusted his posture and took a small bow. "I hope everyone is eager to see something horrific tonight! My name is Linus and I'll be your guide through the museum of carnage you're about to enter. Now, I know what you're thinking! Mr. Linus, why do we need a guide to enter a haunted house? Well, what you're about to see is something more than a haunted house, kiddos. If you're not careful, you may end up being a part of the building as much as I am, or the sights inside, or even the crew." He gestured to a couple of bodies that stood at the top of the stairs. They were unidentifiable, wearing all black and keeping their faces hidden. "Before we enter, I have a few rules. I know, I know. Ugh, rules! Let's all roll our eyes at the stupid things that keep us from having fun!" he said as he twirled around, arms outstretched. "But you are expected to follow them. One. Don't touch anyone or anything associated with the attraction. Two. Keep with the group at all times. I know there isn't much of one tonight, but you'll need to stick with me if you expect to leave here alive. Three. Do as I say. I could save your life. Four. When in doubt, revert to rule three." Mike raised his hand. Linus pointed and smiled. "A question, I wonder what it is you'll ask, dear hound."

"Are there really things that'll kill us in there? This is just a haunted house, right?" Rachel could hear the nervousness in his voice. Allen rubbed along his partner's back and kissed his cheek.

"Scared already, babe?" he teased.

Linus chucked briefly and motioned for the group to

follow him. "Nothing will kill you in here, kind hound. That is, if you follow the rules you were given. If you don't, well I'm afraid I can't tell where your soul will go within the confines of this home."

"He's putting on a good show, Mike. Don't make his job harder than it is," Rachel said, jabbing him in the ribs with her elbow. Mike just stayed silent.

"Well, if there are no further questions, let's take a trip to hell, shall we?" the goat said as he led the group of the steps and into the home.

Old. Decrepit. The words could not define what Rachel first saw upon entering. To her, it felt old, dusty. The rug they gathered on in the foyer was about as clean as a motel carpet. The walls were covered in a lavender floral wallpaper. As she scanned the pattern, Rachel thought it never left the seventies. The floors creaked as they wandered in. Mike stepped on a couple of the boards intentionally to check the strength of their structure, afraid he would fall through.

The door closed behind them and locked. The group could hear the lock echo in the walls of the haunted house. "Now that we are all inside, you will not be able to leave. Those doors will not unlock until the tour is over. Fortunately, we won't have to go far to find hell," Linus said as he opened the first room of the house. As they peered inside, Rachel could make out the interior of a car. A blue neon hue was hovering over the whole insides of the visually deceptive room. Deceptive because Rachel couldn't not believe she was actually seeing a car's view. Though she could see through the windshield, she could not believe that it was daylight, or that the trees were already so dead. Before she could say anything, Linus started to speak. "Step inside, everyone; we really like to throw you into the chaos here," he said as he pushed the group into the first haunt.

HELL ON A TWO-LANE BLACKTOP

The bar radio played Creedence lowly in the background. Kurt swayed around with whomever would put their hands on his hips. The fox's eyes hung low, nearing his nose, yet his exhaustion didn't stop him from enjoying the dirty country rhythms sifting through the drunks. His violet fur glowed under the dim bar lights. After one man stuffed his hand down the back of his tight shorts, he blinked his tired, yellow eyes and nodded to the bathroom. Kurt took his newfound partner, the door creaking open as the stranger pushed the slim, tightly clothed fox against the graffiti-stained walls and pushed his tongue inside.

Rick sat at the end of the empty bar, his darkened blue fur barely visible under the low lights. Rick stuffed a handful of nachos in his mouth, cheese sticking to the lighter blue of his chin and lips, his fingers matted with grease. The blue panda was gulping each sharp tortilla chip down as if it were his last eating contest and this was the finish line. Beneath the slow twangs of the music, the bartender heard Rick's throat choke, then a large sigh of relief escaped it as the mess poured downward. Rick grabbed a handful of napkins and wiped the mess off his fingers and mouth, then pushed it back to the bartender. "Where's all the hot tail in this joint, Sheila?"

The bunny turned around, her khaki fur ruffling underneath her tight pink maternity shirt. Her ears hung low behind her head, draping down to her ass, her belly nearly exposed. Sheila set her yellow eyes on the blue panda, her eyebrow half-cocked. "Rick, ain't no one here who wanna hop on your dick," she said, pouring a beer into a glass and slamming it down. She pushed it towards him, and he pushed it back.

"You know I don't drink and drive, sweetheart." Rick pushed the empty nacho basket towards her, his napkins piled on top.

Sheila rolled her eyes and pointed them behind the bar. "Then why come to a bar, crackhead? I got half a mind to break this bottle over your head and throw you out."

Rick put his hands up in defense. "Hey, I pay for my shit. 'sides, I come here for the food."

"Tony is the worst cook on this fuckin' planet, and you come here for the food? Shit, I bet if he cooked a pile of scat, you'd eat the damn thing."

Rick clicked his tongue and opened his hands wide, "Only the lord knows that, sweetheart. Guess we'll have to find out one day if he ever does." Sheila only rolled her eyes in response.

Kurt moaned violently as his dance partner rammed into him. The stall shook, screws nearly ripping from the dingy walls. His partner's moans grew higher; the fox knew they were close. He didn't wonder if anyone heard them; he only grew tired of waiting for the orgasm to fill him. "C'mon, fill me up!" the fox grunted, stroking himself. He repeated it over, and over, nearly begging for the end. He had shot his load moments before; everything at that moment was merely playing nice. Kurt didn't even know who was behind him anymore. The bar could have run a train on his tight ass, and his brain wouldn't have registered it. His head bounced; he could feel his brain move like sludge in his skull. He closed his eyes, and when he opened them, his anonymous fuck was gone.

Kurt's hands fiddled with his clothes. He stared at the mirror, smoothing any matted fur he could see and staggered from the restroom. The slender fox slammed his body against the bar. He tried to take a seat, but failed, falling hard on the floor. Taking a moment, the young guy lifted himself up, his arms shaking, then finally secured his ass on the seat. Rick's eyes stared Kurt up and down. The blue panda was drawn to the boy's long, brown hair and how it matched his orange fur. His eyes traveled along the curves of the fox's hips, and he grunted when he took a long stop at his ass. The fox's tail flicked as he stared back. The newcomer gave him a wink then turned his attention to the bartender. "Hey, you know where I can get a ride home?" The words slurred from his mouth lazily. The fox leaned his head on the bar as if the alcohol was making his head heavy and he needed to support it.

Sheila's ears swayed as she nodded her head in disappointment. "Boy, I am not your mama. You can call a goddamn cab at the payphone outside."

Rick moved his hand forward and interjected, "Say, now, wait a minute. What's your name, kid?" He leaned over, turning his attention to the fox. His blue fur nearly stood on edge, eager to jump into the fox's pants.

The fox lifted his head slightly, smiled a bit at the blue panda. "Kurt." He tried to keep from saying much more for fear of all the night's endeavors spilling up from his gut and onto the floor.

"Well, Kurt, say I give you a lift home. What's in it for

this ol' panda?" He cocked his eyebrow, a smile traveling far across his face.

Kurt lifted his head fully, smiling wryly at the blue panda. He let a hand travel onto Rick's leg, stopping right at his inner thigh and squeezing firmly. "I'd make it worth your while."

Rick turned his head to Sheila and winked at her, "No one to hop on my dick, huh?"

Sheila scoffed and turned away. Rick took his new companion and led him to his car. Their feet sloshed through the hard dirt and gravel parking lot. Rick turned his head upward. "No moon tonight. The perfect kind of sky for drivin'."

"Is that your car?" Kurt said lazily. Rick couldn't tell if it was disappointment or disbelief. He huffed at the question either way.

"You don't know your cars. This baby here is a 1969 Pontiac GTO. Fastest bitch alive. Runs them clunker Mustangs off the road and owns it."

Kurt stood staring at the old model car, rolling his eyes. "You're like my dad, lecturing me about this shit. What's with the paint job anyways?" His voice grew firm as he eyed the car's slick black paint and red hood. He walked around to the front of the car and put his fingers on the deep crimson, a claw tracing over the giant cock dripping pre etched into the paint.

"Biggest, baddest bitch in town." Rick let the comment hang in the air as he opened the passenger side door, waving his hands to usher the fox inside. Kurt didn't waste any time by jumping in, eager to get home and sleep off the beers he had guzzled down. Rick hopped in on his side and sped off. The wicked demon of a car roared as it spun out of the lot and veered left. The fox gripped at his seat, not expecting the quick shot out.

"Whoa, man. I didn't even tell you where I lived!" he shouted, trying to talk over the engine's vigorous noise. Rick shook his head and placed a hand on the fox's thigh.

"Did I guess right?" The fox only responded with a nod, indicating he had. Rick stepped on the pedal, pushing his car to go faster, well over the speed limit; the demon took the road as if it were its own. As he drove, Rick unzipped his pants and let his cock fly out. "Why don't you work on that compensation. My throb knob could use some attention, honey."

Uneasy at the speed they were going, Kurt hesitated. First only putting his hand on the man's shaft and stroking lightly. The car took a hard curve, forcing Kurt to nearly hit his window. "Whoa, man. Can you, like, slow it the fuck down?"

"It's all right. I've done this before. Now get back to work. Nobody rides for free in this baby." Still uneasy, the drunken fox pushed his head down the blue panda's shaft. The car sped faster, pushing well over 100 mph. Rick's cock stood firm, adrenaline pumping through his veins, and a hot piece of ass on his dick. He couldn't have asked for a better night.

Kurt's nose burned at the scent of the panda's musk. A wave of disgust washed over his body at the stench. He didn't know how much longer he could handle it. He shut his eyes, almost torturing himself to push through, hoping the guy would cum quick. Kurt shot up, not able to handle the stench any longer, "Dude, when's the last time you showered?" Rick didn't say anything, as he sped down the long, narrow roads of C.R. 15. "Where even are we?"

"The bar's about forty-five minutes away from any town. You should know that, since you were there. Don't you got work to be doin'?"

The fox shook his head, "I can't, man. When's the last time you washed that thing?"

Rick slammed on his brakes, forcing the fox to ram his

head into the windshield. Kurt left a large web of shattered glass along the surface. Rick sped up again only to slam hard and veer around to the opposite direction. Kurt's head slammed into the passenger window, blood splattering across it. The fox groaned wearily. His hands rubbed along his head, the pain surging through. He tried to look around the car to get his surroundings. "Wha—" The blue panda jammed his knife into Kurt's throat. As he sped down the empty road, he twisted the blade, playing with his victim. Blood sputtered from the wound, then slowly oozed from the fox's mouth. Kurt could feel himself slipping into the darkness, the view of the starless night pouring out of his eyes.

Rick left the blade inside, grabbing his toy by the head and shoving his mouth over his thick member. His demon screeched down each sharp curve, tires thrusting away from the asphalt as he took the hills as his own. "FUCK! That is what I'm talkin' 'bout!" he screamed, his seed mixing with Kurt's blood as he emptied himself in the body's muzzle. He let the carcass rest in his lap as he sped maniacally through the night, engine roaring without fear. He rolled his window down, took in the gusts of air slamming in his face. "Now I gotta find someone new to play with."

The asphalt burned as she stuck her thumb out. The vixen hated herself for having black fur, sun pummeling her body as she tried to get a lift from anyone who would save her from the broken down car she sat on. Her sunglasses covered most of her faded fur, eyes narrowing as she finally saw a car. "Oh shit yea!" she exclaimed, hopping from her car. Her hands waived violently, hoping she would be seen by the stranger approaching her.

Rick's beast slowed to a crawl as his eyes narrowed in on this new victim. Windows already rolled down, he pulled up beside her. "Car trouble?"

Tracey nodded her head, an angered smile clenching her lips shut as he waved her hand to her car. "You think you could give me a ride? I don't have any money, but I really need the lift. This sun is killing me!" She could feel the desperation in her voice, hoping he wouldn't be an asshole and let her in. Rick only nodded. Tracey squealed as he opened the door, not noticing the blood on his seats from the night before.

"Next town's only a few minutes away," the red panda with blue fur coating his body said as he stepped on the gas and sped off. Her hands grabbed onto whatever they could find as he drove wildly on the empty road. Not prepared for the speeds they were reaching, her nails dug deep into the car's interior. Tracey closed her eyes as the car spun to a turn, tires squealing like a pig being gutted. Her ears twitched as she heard gravel spitting up from behind them; she knew they had turned off of the major road and started to get anxious. The vixen flattened the pink tank that hugged her body and slowly opened her eyes to get her bearings. As her vision steadied, she could only see dust and gravel surrounding them as the speedster flew through the off-beaten road. "Why'd we get off the main road?"

Rick simply grunted as he continued down the road, the car throwing the vixen around beneath her seat belt. Her hands grabbed anything they could to steady her, unprepared for the bumpy ride she was enduring to escape the heat.

"Seriously. The next town is back the other way! Why are we here? I will kick your ass!" she screamed, lunging out and digging her claws into the panda's arm. Rick flung his arm over and grabbed her by her head, slamming it down against the dashboard repeatedly.

"Fuckin bitch!" he yelled back, his voice growling as each letter left his tongue. A scream leaped from her throat in short staccato breaths with each hit. She tried punching her hands against him, hitting her attacker as hard as she was able. She clawed at his arms, grabbed the back of his hand, anything she could do to free herself from him.

Frustrated, Rick spun his car in a circle to force her to lose any control she had of her body. As the car came to a full screeching stop, her hands lunged for her seatbelt. Freeing herself, she grunted and tried to push him off of him. She flung one hand behind her to open the door, and when it thrust open, her body flew from her seat and down onto the hard gravel. Rocks pierced her back and arms, the burning gravel stinging her fur. Tracey didn't hesitate, her hands waving through the dirt. She pushed her leg back until she was able to get up, but Rick was quick, slamming his foot into her gut, forcing a large breath from lungs and into the air. He lifted her up and threw her on the hood of his car, her back landing hard on the shaft of the painted cock. Still trying to wriggle free, he slammed his fist into her gut again. With more air escaping her, Tracey curled up on the hood of his car as he grabbed his knife and flattened her out once more. He jammed the knife into her gut, twisting it playfully. Screeching now, she lost the strength to fight him off. "Fuck!" she screamed out, her heart raging against her chest. "You fucking bastard!" the words spat out, saliva splattering in his face.

Rick pulled the knife out of her, licking the blade clean. He let out a gruff chuckle from his belly and stuffed the knife into his back pocket, leaving her on his car. Tracey covered her wound, blood oozing from her gut, staining her hands as she tried to apply what little pressure she could. Tears slithered down her face; she could no longer hold them in as the pain pulsed through her body. Weakened wails seeped from her teeth as he hopped back into his car, slamming the door shut. The car still running, he revved up the engine and sped back, forcing her to fly off the hood. Tracey's screams became hoarse, her voice all but gone. He revved up again, the car jolting forward a moment. Tracey kicked rocks towards the car, but never reached it. Their eyes locked like two fires feeding each other's flames as he sped towards her. "Motherfucker!" she screamed, throwing every bit of gravel she could at her oncoming death.

In a flash, the car rammed into her, tires crushing every bone they touched. Blood splattered underneath the car as her skeleton was forced from her fur, poking through every inch of her arms. Teeth flung from her muzzle as her jaw was demolished by the weighty vehicle. Rick ran over her body a few times, tires catching what flesh it could with each impact. When he finished, he got out of his car and stared at the job he had finished. A smile traveled far across his face, his tail flicking behind him. He knelt down, pushing his hand into the corpse destroyed on the gravel, then stared off in the distance, eager for another victim.

Liam sped his Challenger into the gas station. His forest-covered knuckles stretched over the steering wheel. His tires screeched as they met the uneven parking lot, the car kicking from his fast wheels. The wolf smoothed the green fur of his arms when he parked it, stretching his neck as if he had been driving across two states. He ran a hand along the darker green of his chin, then popped out of his speed machine.

Rick sat in his car, waiting for the tank to fill. He hated waiting outside, though the trips were always short enough. He guzzled the remains of his gas station pizza the moment the tank clicked signaling he was all full. Like a second-class gentleman, he wiped his grease-ridden hands on a couple of napkins, then dropped the trash on the floor. Liam saw the make of Rick's car and started to mosey around, whistling as if it were a hot young thing looking for love.

"That's a pretty big dick on your hood; people might think you're compensating for something," Liam's low

Southern drawl oozed from his mouth. His eyes narrowed on the blue panda.

Rick shook the nozzle before removing it from his car and returning it to the tank. His eyes focused on the lean wolf. He studied the definition of the wolf's stomach, seeing the toned, slim muscles underneath his tight black shirt. His eyes slowly curved upward, following the mixtures of light and dark green of man in front of him. "It's an homage," he answered swiftly.

"An homage to what, the last dick you sucked?"

Rick's blood began to swirl inside him. He wanted to smash the wolf's skull down on the pavement. He wanted skull fragments to spit from his fur. He wanted to see how small of a brain this wolf had.

"Yo babe, how much am I putting in this bitch?" a voice called from behind the gas tank. A small, brown kitten emerged. Rick's eyes zeroed in, first studying the cat's short hair, the bangs curving to the side, his square glasses, and light chocolate fur. He exhaled a large breath, fighting the standing ovation that was fighting his tight pants. The kitten's tight shorts accentuated the curve of his ass, driving the carnal desires of the panda.

"However much cash we got, Mason. I'm sure we're good for a few bucks, and a few fucks," Liam responded, pulling the kitten in and kissing him slightly on the lips.

Rick peered around and noticed the classic car sitting on the other side. "What year is she?"

Liam smacked the cat on the ass then turned to Rick. He smoothed his hand over his head, "1971. I wanted white, but settled for the red. She's one beauty of a car. She'll leave anyone in the dust; don't even have to drive her."

The red panda smirked, the blue and white of his fur stretching wide with his lips. "Sounds like that's a challenge."

"Takes a lot of balls to challenge me."

They stood across from each other, eyes like two separate fires adding fuel to each other's twisted ego. "Well, I got mine painted on my car; think they're big enough to take you down?"

Liam stepped forward as if to say mine's bigger. He put a hand on his hip. "You're such an easy kill, man. I could kick your ass on the road while fuckin' the hot tail ridin' with me."

"Then own up to it. I bet my bitch could pass you up quicker than lightning." Rick's voice grew fierce. He wanted to demolish Liam on the road. He wanted to beat him in the race then watch his body get crushed by the car he drove. He stared the man down, tail flicking behind him in excitement as flashes of blood and fur painted the road.

Liam scoffed at Rick's statement then nodded to the empty highway. "See you in five."

The two drivers lined up their cars side by side, the black demon and the crimson devil revving madly as they stared through each other. The wolf's boyfriend leaned over and started to unzip his pants. Mason slid his paw around Liam's shaft, and, as he took a firm grip, the two devils sped off. Mason pulled his body over and started to ride his tongue along the wolf's hardened member; Liam stepped on the gas and started to pass up the black devil. A smile traveled across Rick's face as they both took a hard curve, tires spinning flawlessly as the metal nearly touched. They sped tightly next to each other, yet Liam was slightly ahead of the red panda. Before long, Rick started to get tired of the race, pulling his car away from the classic Challenger, then ramming his car into the deep red paint.

"Fuck!" Liam screamed. Mason lifted his head to see what happened before the wolf pushed him back down. "I'll take care of this; just don't leave me hangin'!" Rick slammed his car into Liam's again, this time making him lose control. Tires squealed as he skidded off and into the empty pasture next to them. Liam turned his wheel violently into the skid in hopes of minimizing the damage, yet the force was enough to lift his car slightly. Clods of grass and dirt spit out from the wheels as he forced his engine to speed out of the green entrapment. His car jumped off the ground as he pummeled back onto the road and away. They drove until Rick's car was out of sight from the rear mirror. "Jesus fuck!" Liam shouted again, driving his way towards anything, everything just to be away from the panda. Mason lifted his head finally, turning his hair away from his face and wiping the seed from his mouth. "Forgot you were down there."

The cat smacked his brown paw against Liam's shoulder, then sat back in his seat. "What the fuck just happened?"

"I dunno. We were winning, and I guess he couldn't take the loss so he started to push us off," Liam said as he slowed his damaged devil and pulled over. He sat back in against his hard, leather seat trying to calm his heart. The sun beamed over them, the wolf almost seeing it rise off the asphalt. Mason opened the glove compartment, pulling out a small caliper gun and ensuring it was loaded. "Babe, we don't..."

"We don't know if he's coming back!" Mason shouted before Liam could finish his statement. "At least we'll have something." He turned his gaze outside of his window.

"Listen, he won't come back. He was just some nut job; we're clear now." Liam leaned over and pulled the cat into his arms. He kissed him on his forehead. "I got you," he said, his voice slightly hoarse from coming off the adrenaline high, a small wink jumping off his face. Yet Mason was still uneasy. The unnerving force wouldn't leave his chest. He tried breathing deeply, yet the sense of panic would not settle. His dark brown hand clutched the light brown of his chest fur and tight shirt. Liam held him tighter, taking the gun from his boyfriend. He gripped it tight, ready for anyone who wanted to fuck with his cat.

"Let's get out of…" A sudden force slammed into the crimson devil. Liam fired the gun upon impact, the bullet blowing through the door. The wolf slammed his head into the window. Mason hit the dashboard as their car was pushed far up the road. Quick to leave consciousness, their bodies fell entangled in each other on the seats.

"Looks like you're in a bitch of a place to be!" Rick shouted from behind them, driving every bit of strength into their now beat-up Challenger. His own car took a huge chunk of carnage, yet the panda didn't care. He threw their car forward a few feet. The tires left dark skid marks on the road as it tried to resist being forced to move. Sun beaming down on them, Rick thrust open his door and set foot onto the burning asphalt. His feet could feel the imaginary flames beneath him, yet he trudged forward. His dark blue fur glowed beneath the afternoon light as his hand pulled the driver side door and pulled Liam's heavy, unconscious body from the vehicle. Rick's blood dripped down from his head, his body starting to show signs of damage from his actions. The wolf's body made a hard thud as he was dropped to the ground, then his shoes started to grind being dragged to the back of his competitor's car. Bits of green fur flew from the wolf's limber body as Rick started to strip him of his clothes. In moments Liam was exposed to the heat and fire of the elements. Rick smoothed his hand over his victim's chest, feeling the definition of Liam's chest and abs. Smiling, he pulled the wolf's arms above his head.

Rick grabbed a bit of rope from his car. Before returning to the wolf, he glared to see if Mason had woken up. The panda scoffed at the boy in the car, still knocked out from his impact. He let him alone and started to tie Liam's hands to the bumper of his car. When he was satisfied it would hold, he hopped in his car and started it up. The demon roared upon firing. Rick took a moment, thinking it would take a few tries, but impressed at how quick his prized speed demon awoke upon being called. The red panda adjusted himself, stepping on the gas to roar the engine again yet remaining in park. He let it roar wildly on the empty road.

The wolf slowly started to come to. His vision blurred at first, but quickly he started shouting as he felt the heat beneath him. "What the fuck! What the fuck, man! Where's my fucking clothes!" The wolf's body trembled against the car as his head darted to the road beneath him, then to the sky. The blue above swallowed his vision as he tried to dart his eyes around the empty fields surrounding him. "C'mon, man! It was just a loss! You don't have to kill me, man!" His words shook from his tongue, breathing rapid. The wolf's lungs pounded against his chest; he felt they would burst at any moment—hoped they would burst, that they would kill him before Rick would start driving. The anticipation of feeling his body torn wildly by asphalt and dirt made him ache, taking over the burning sensation boiling beneath him. "Fuck!" he shouted once more, knowing he wasn't going to get out of it.

As Rick heard his victim wake, he sped off. Liam's cries sung loud, his body tearing. He tried everything to wriggle his hands free, dislocating his arms in the process. His ankle snapped. The wolf had never endured so much pain before, and Rick wasn't about to stop. Blood started to paint the road like tire imprints from a car losing control. He pushed his car faster, driving until Liam's body started to tear open, his lower body being left behind and intestines spilling over the road.

He only made it as far as a couple miles before stopping quickly and swerving the car in the opposite direction. The body swung hard after hitting the demon's frame. When the wails of his victim finally ceased, Rick knew he was dead, yet he kept the body hitched a moment longer to obliterate every bit of the man. He drove his car, watching the bits of flesh and fur fly behind him. Soon, the mixtures of blood and green fur meshed with the oceanic sky. A heavy laugh burst from his mouth as the dopamine shot through his brain. He loved every bit of carnage he was leaving behind him. He wanted more. More blood. More flesh. He wanted to soak the whole blackened asphalt with his prey's body. It drove him wild, the kind of wild you feel when you're playing poker and you have the best hand at the table, and you know you're going to win the whole pile of cash while crushing every schmuck that came for you.

"I am the fucking Superbeast!" he screamed out of the window. He took one last look behind him, seeing the blood was gone. The red panda inhaled deeply, smelling the metallic air. He rubbed his blue paw over his head, then down to his crotch. "Rock fucking hard!" the words charged out of his muzzle with a hefty laugh as he sped onward.

In the distance, the crimson devil sat in its damage, yet the cat had finally awakened. He stood in the middle of the road, gun aimed at the black devil. "Son of a bitch!" he shouted, firing the only rounds he had on him, but the Devil kept going. Each bullet hit a random spot, one in the lights, another on the hood. The final bullet burst through Rick's windshield, hitting hard in his chest.

"Fuck!" he screamed, not accustomed to having a piece of lead forced into his body. The blue fur of his hand meshed with his blood as he clutched at the wound on his chest. The ground squealed as the tires skidded off the road. With one arm, he tried to regain control, but couldn't steer his vehicle back. The Devil rode wildly through the field, ramming through tall grass and dirt. In a quick shot of a second, the car slammed into a tree. Branches quaked as if hurricane winds hit them. Before he could leave the car, the branches fell heavily, glass shattering like bone. Fragments poured over the hood and into the car; the roof collapsed down onto Rick's head, splitting him open. In that moment of madness, Mason waited. He waited to see if the deranged killer would rise one last time, and when the wind soothed the bruises on his arms he decided he was finally free from the calamity. Another burst of the earth's breath hit his lean stomach, forcing a large wail to escape his mouth. His body wouldn't hold much longer; his knees buckled, then he collapsed to the ground.

His eyes wanted to let rain fall from his face, yet all he could manage were dry heaves of pain and anguish. Each cry that escaped him grew louder—a syncopated pain that beat his whole body inside. Helpless, he left himself exposed to the road, hoping someone would drive by and rip him from the perversion of death unleashed upon him and his boyfriend. "Liam!" a long, pained moan roared from his belly and from his lips. He didn't want to understand how much he'd lost in those few short moments of his life. He didn't want any of it to be real. His mind raced with thoughts of it being all a nightmare; a momentary lapse of pure dreaming forcing him to live out any absurd fears in this world. Yet it was all real. The asphalt he lay upon was just as real as the bullet he shot through the strange madman.

In all his mourning, he never sensed Rick's presence behind him. Before the cat could smell the panda's stench, Rick grabbed him by his hair. Mason screamed between his sobs, trying to get back the will to fight, but his body only offered weak slaps and pushes. Rick grabbed the gun from his victim, driving it hard across Mason's face. His body was flung away by the impact. The gun drove through his jaw, wrenching his whole torso away from his killer. Teeth flew from his mouth as he landed on the road. He took the gun and tossed it aside. "I'm still alive, bitch," he said with a gruff anger bubbling in his throat, and, before Mason could hoist himself up and run, Rick jumped on his body. He pulled his knife from his back pocket.

Mason threw his arms against the red panda, pummeling his chest until he found the bullet wound. Barely able to scream, he let out a quick "fuck" and pressed his thumb inside of the area.

"Fucking bitch!" Rick screamed back at the cat beneath him, taking his knife and driving it hard into Mason's right eye. He twisted the blade around, scooping it from its socket and throwing it aside.

The cat was fortunate Rick hadn't driven it deeper. Taking all his strength, he drove his fingers inside of the panda's wound again. He pushed them so far deep he could feel the bones of his rib cage. He wriggled them around, trying to deepen the damage he dealt. Adrenaline pumping through his veins, he did everything to push the pain from his face and get the man off him. His leg shot up quick, landing in Rick's balls. The red panda shouted again, losing his grip on his victim. The moment Mason saw the out, he jumped up and pushed the man off. As if shouting to the gods above, he unleashed every painful, angered cry from his throat and started to beat the red panda. Punches landed on his face and chest, and when he could no longer hold the knife, Mason seized it and drove it hard into his attacker's chest. He stabbed over, and over, not caring where it went. He just wanted the man dead. He wanted the man to suffer what he suffered, what Liam suffered.

When Rick finally went limp, Mason delivered a final stab, leaving the knife in his chest. With the rest of his strength, he hoisted himself up, all the pain coming rushing back to him. He couldn't take the sheer force of it. Falling back to the ground, he held his hands to his eye, crying madly as all his senses were attacked in a quick barrage of pain. He took as many deep breaths as he could, hoisting himself up again, and limped to his car. He didn't wait to see if the man was alive. He forced the keys of Liam's crimson devil and made a few attempts to start it up. On the third try, it woke, and, without thinking, he shifted the gear and sped away. He didn't look back; he just drove. He drove as far away as he could, blood oozing from his socket. He didn't care about the damage of the car, the bumper left behind. He just wanted out. He wanted to be free, and he was finally able to taste it after being at war for so long.

INTERLUDE 1

Rachel moved her hands over the ground as the group came to. Like waking up from after a night of drinking, she moved her body and tried to lift her head. She let her eyes linger for a moment, trying to steady the dizziness that was consuming her vision, and after moments of waiting, she saw she was in a normal room of the house. Her friends were all returning to consciousness as well.

Mike groaned as he rolled his hefty body over. His vision suffering the same as Rachel's, he took a moment to try and settle his body. He found his boyfriend draped over his legs, the wolf clinging to one as he finally came to. The pair looked at each other for a brief moment, trying to figure out what had just happened to the group. Allen moved in for a small kiss, as he brought back feelings of terror from what he just witnessed; from what the group just witnessed.

"Did anyone else feel that?" she asked as Allen was helping up the bulky basset hound. The wolf ran his fingers over his head as if a headache were settling in, the lights illuminating his dismal grey fur. The slender wolf stared at the painting, studying every detail that stood in front of them. He started to feel the same fear as well, but tried to shake it off as all part of the act. He clung to Mike, kissed him on the cheek and spoke up.

"What the fuck did we sign up for, Rach?" he asked, but he knew he wouldn't get an answer. Rachel knew about as much as he did in that moment.

Mike let his eyes wander as he started to settle down. He could feel his body expanding with each breath he took in, his ears listening to each inhalation. There was a feeling in his gut telling him the ride was far from over. Deep down he could feel something dangerous in this house, something unnatural. Though he wondered what wicked menagerie was planned ahead, he took in a deep breath to remain calm. "Let's just keep going; I don't think we experienced anything real, or anything that could hurt us," Mike tried to reason. Rachel thought his face was drooping more than usual as she stared at him.

"I'm sure you're right, but I'm still creeped out," she responded swiftly. Rachel had a sickening feeling, too. She wondered if the trio was experiencing the same feeling of discomfort as they sat in the empty room. They stared at each other, though none could assume what the other was thinking. Rachel started to feel isolated, unable to find a way to communicate to her friends. Allen remained close to his boyfriend. He didn't want to let the basset hound go, and as fear started to tremble through his bones, he felt he would be alone soon.

Linus entered, his step quietly moving into the center to check on his guests. Rachel noticed he always kept his back straight, as if to carry himself as a noble, or a priest, or someone with an ego larger than the rest of the world's. His body didn't bounce as he walked. Rachel watched as his twig-like legs stepped away from his body. The moment she saw his smile, a shiver of fear ran through her body. He waved his hands and bowed before them. "I trust you found your first experience frightening?" His voice loomed on the final word of his question.

"How did the painting do that?" Rachel asked as she passed their guide. She knew something touched her. She knew the painting was more than what she saw in that room. She felt as if she were inside it, inside the story, witnessing an act so devastating she almost feared for her own life.

The goat cocked his head slightly and responded, "Do what, exactly?" His eyes squinted as the words left his mouth. Rachel hated how the pentagram was etched on his forehead. *How cheesy can a dude be? Seriously,* she thought to herself as she searched for the words to respond.

"Y'know. Touch us, play like a movie. It all seemed like we were right there." The lioness was starting to shake, but followed their guide further into the home. She couldn't seem to find the right words to describe what happened with the painting. She had never experienced being pulled into another world before, and she hoped she would never have to do it again.

The goat chuckled. "Oh, darling, I believe that's all part of the act. Some secrets of our trade just can't be revealed, I'm afraid. As you progress through the house, your experiences will get more daring. More dangerous. More frightening. They may not all be paintings. You may have someone tell you their story. Or...you may become the story. Carnage is a home of terrors that are ever changing. You all are here at the perfect time, too! The horrors you're about to see will not remain for long. A new bunch of perversions is being acquired after we finish tonight." Though the hall looked long, the walk was short. The trio was met with more of the same dank lavender walls. It started to make Mike ill the more he watched it pass by him. Before he could muster the courage to say anything, the group stopped and there were three ways ahead of them.

"How often do you change things up?" Allen asked, his curiosity jabbing his brain as he stared at their guide.

Linus smiled as he his eyes focused on the boy in front of him. His teeth were gritting down against each other as he waved his hand. "Why, we evolve every decade or so. Some horrors are so enticing, the audience can't wait to return to the party." The goat turned around and looked at each. "Each of you must choose a path. The first hall is The Unrevealed. As if led blind through darkness, the ones who take this hall will be forced to confront the image of uncertainty. The second hall before you is the hall of Abscondence. Pushed through unescapable tasks, you'll be confronted with fierce horrors forcing you to want to escape. Choose this hall and know that you'll need to plunge hard into what you see. The third hall is the hall of Absolution. Forced to confront hauntings unimaginable to most individuals, you'll be confronted with madness and the struggle of letting go. A guide will be assigned to each one, but your journey from here will be made alone until the end of our tour. Choose wisely." The last two words echoed amongst them.

"What happens if we don't?" Rachel asked, unsure if she really wanted to do the rest of the trip on her own.

"Then you'll have to leave," the goat said sternly. Linus knew the crew would stick to the tour. He was, however, prepared to kill anyone who wanted to leave the event early. *Carnage is not in the habit of letting its prey run free from its mouth*, the goat thought to himself as he waited for the trio to answer.

They looked between themselves. "It's just a haunted house. We're not really going to die. I say we do it," Mike said while grabbing his wolf's ass. "I'm starting to have a bit of fun; let's get on with it!" He was quick to push. Mike tried to ignore his gut feeling. The basset hound wanted to run headfirst into whatever was coming his way. He was ready to conquer the house and leave unscathed. Rachel could see a sense of wonder in his eyes, a sense she had never seen before.

She looked over at Allen and he shrugged. "If he goes, I go, even if we split up." The wolf walked up to the entrance of the first hall. Allen stared down the entryway, trying to get a sense of what he was in for. Most of the hall was consumed by darkness, the same peeling wallpaper as the rest of the house; the same filthy carpeted marron floors. "What's down there?" he asked, a short burst of fear entangled in his voice as he looked at Linus. The goat guide turned his head slightly, eyes narrowing the slender, grey wolf.

"It's the unknown for a reason, darling. But if it's a landmark you're looking for, I'm told from past visitors that the abyss is darker than the escape. Weed your way through the blackness; you won't know what's on the other side until you get there." Linus waved his hand before turning to the rest of the group. A cloaked figure stood before him with a torch. It said nothing, only moving its hand to gesture moving forward.

The basset hound looked over the remaining two halls, stroking his chin on which to choose. A green neon light flushed on from the Hall of Abscondence. His eyes fixated on the bright glow, seeing unfinished floors that looked as if they would break the moment you stepped on them. The purple wallpaper was peeling; his stomach turned at the sickening radiance emerging from the walls. There was something venomous about the hallway. His stomach pushed him to stay back, but he was driven to move forward. His mind was set, telling his body to suck it up and move. He started to walk up to the green neon, his eyes seeing framed paintings along the hall. "I'll take this one. How scary can it be?" Mike said, shrugging his shoulders as he looked over at their guide. His nose twitched as he started the smell the scent of old blood. He looked back down the corridor and saw the walls stained, blood splattered across old purple as his eyes scanned each picture. He didn't notice at first, but each frame held a layer of blood around it. He let the fear emerge in his chest before moving his body and shaking it away.

Linus smiled and walked up the basset hound. "I'm sure you'll find the hunger exhumed from this hall exhilarating. Just be sure not to let the evils inside devour you. Your remains aren't always digested," he said with a laugh. Mike didn't quite understand, but proceeded to move forward anyway. Another cloaked figure gestured quietly as they moved into the neon.

Mike turned around and waved to Rachel. "See you on the other side, Rach!" She rolled her eyes at his enthusiasm. Fear was starting to crawl up her body, but she felt she had to move on. Her friends had gone in, and she was not going to live it down if they knew she didn't take on the third hall. She lifted her hand and gave a faint wave back, saying nothing as he slowly grew out of sight.

"I suppose that leaves the Hall of Absolution, then," Rachel said with a heavy sigh. A light flushed on as she approached it. A wave of smoke started to linger in the air the longer she stared down the lengthy corridor. The hall was dressed differently than the others. She noticed the ceiling caved in, fiberglass hanging from the holes she would have to pass by. She could already feel her fur itching at the thought of breezing by the cotton-like material. Unfinished floors led the way to a door, but her eyes couldn't see what was on it. Pool cues and empty beer steins lay on the ground; her nose cringed at the smell of stale alcohol that stained the cement.

The goat smiled at her. "That is easily the hardest hall for most of our guests. Are you sure, darling?" Without giving it a second thought, she nodded her head. "Very well, then; I'll be your guide for this hall." She looked at him, his smile making her sick as she started to follow Linus through the dilapidated entrance. "Don't get lost, dear. It's easy to get stuck in a single hall. Your eyes don't always tell you what's before you, and some illusions are dangerous. If you emerge from the hell you're entering, you'll be wholly incomplete, a new you missing a piece of you."

The lioness said nothing in return, walking directly behind Linus. "Fuck," she cursed under her breath. "What the fuck did I get myself into?" she asked herself as they traveled passed the first crater in the ceiling.

Linus turned his head around, leaving his body straight forward as they walked. "I'm afraid there's no going back now." He started to laugh, a slow, curdling laugh that pierced the lioness' ears. Rachel didn't know what would lie ahead of her, but she had no choice but to finish the night, much like her friends.

THE UNREVEALED

Allen's eyes glowed in the darkness. His body started to tense up the further into the dark he went. His eyes scanned over the walls surrounding him. He tried to get a feel for the guide leading him in the unknown, but the figure was just that, a figure. He wondered if it would speak to him as they walked. "I guess he wasn't joking when he said we'd be blind, heh," the wolf said nervously. His hands brushed through his grey fur. He watched it leave a trail behind him as it left his body. The beat of his heart started to rise the moment he realized he was just a slender twig in darkness. The wind could cut him in half and no one would notice in the abyss. "We don't actually die from this, right? I mean, you guys don't kill us?" His voice was shaky. He wanted some reassurance he would make it out alive, but the guide said nothing. "Hey, do you even talk?" he asked, trying to reach for the guide's shoulder, but it only sped up.

Panic was starting to rise through his body. He started to realize the torch was getting farther away. Allen moved as fast as he could, picking his feet up and trying to reach the guide, but the fire was getting dimmer, and the guide farther. "Hey, wait up!" he shouted ahead, but the guide did nothing. It kept moving faster down the hall. Allen had never had to run so fast before, his breath leaving his body quickly with each heavy step down the corridor. It wasn't long before it was enveloped in complete darkness. "You fucker! I said wait—" His foot tripped, forcing the wolf to fall hard through the hall. Screaming, Allen felt he was falling through a hole, as if it were all a dream, only he wouldn't wake up at the end of it. If his body ever hit the floor, he feared he would die. He plunged further reaching out for something, anything, yet there was only darkness around him. His heart raged against his chest while the fear of what lay below him overtook his body. The wolf clenched his eye tight, not wanting to see the aftermath of the fall; not wanting to see his own death happen before him.

"Stop, stop, STOP!!" he screamed. Like a snap, he felt his body stop. He felt a floor beneath him, his hand trailing along cracks in cement. "What the fuck!" he exclaimed as he jumped from the ground. The shock of still being alive washed over his body as he started to touch his chest and face. Allen chuckled briefly as he slapped his face to ensure he didn't lose consciousness in the fall.

His eyes trailed around him, seeing empty bleachers and a court before him. But as he looked around, he got the sense that he was not the only person here. His body felt surrounded. His fur stiffened the more uneasy he felt. "Where the fuck am I?" The words took a long stroll of his tongue as he tried to see where the guide left him. "I guess they really got me. I gotta tell Rach this shit is legit." He reached for his phone, only to see it didn't have service. "All the fuckin' cell phone towers in this world, and I gotta have no service. I swear I'm canceling this shit when I'm through here," he said as he started to move into the court area. Stadium lights lit up the gym he found himself in. His eyes started to really study how dilapidated the bleachers were, how the roof looked unstable, and the floor dug up. "This place really went to shit. I mean, damn."

"That's what everyone says when they first get here." Allen's eyes darted around the area to find a tall ram standing behind him. A brief yelp escaped his mouth as the grey wolf jumped back a few inches. Allen took a moment to look over the ram's blue fur.

"Who the fuck are you? And why are you so...swol?" Allen's eyes trailed down the ram's body, focusing on the thickness of his muscles, his abs, and his legs. The lights illuminated the fierce blue and dark navy patterns of his fur as the ram stared back at the wolf. Like a blue flame waiting for something to burn, he watched Allen closely as the wolf walked around the towering body before him. Allen noted the ram wore nothing save for a jockstrap as he examined the figure, stopping for a moment to stare at the exposed ass.

"So you chose the Hall of Uncertainty. I doubt you'll have what it takes, but as the gatekeeper here, we'll have to find out," the ram said with a chuckle. He walked around the wolf, sizing him up. His eyes gave a look of disappointment as he saw the fragile body of the wolf that stood before him.

Allen's eyes pierced through the flame before him. "What the fuck does that mean?" The wolf was annoyed, as if someone had pinched too hard; a little sting that would go away in a brief moment, yet still painful when it happens.

"Let's play a game." The ram's voice boomed in the decrepit gymnasium as he sat on the ground. In an instant two cups appeared. The gatekeeper filled one cup with rocks, the other empty and placed them on the ground. His hands moved quickly as he shuffled. Allen watched, though not completely able to follow the motions of the fast flame on the ground. When the ram was finished, he waved his hands over the game. "Take a seat and make a choice. Choose the empty one, and I'll let you pass. Choose the rocks, you'll be held here until I've told my tales." Allen sat before the flame, studying the cups before him. The ram's body snapped close to the wolf, licking Allen's cheek. "Choose wisely; I can get a little out of hand if you pick the wrong cup," the ram whispered in the ear of the wolf.

Allen was shaking now, his hands quaking against his knees as he tried to decide. There was a small breeze in the room with them, something Allen shrugged off as the air conditioner. The longer he thought about this decision, the more he felt something else was watching him. His eyes moved around the room, yet they only caught the air. He blinked swiftly, and for a moment, he thought he saw a crowd of people in the bleachers. The moment he blinked again, they were gone. "Are there spirits with us?" he asked the gatekeeper.

The ram moved his hand, trying to keep the wolf's attention focused on the game. "Make your choice," he said sternly, getting impatient with Allen's inability to choose.

Allen tried to stay focused on the cups before him. He didn't realize how hard of a decision it could be. There were only two cups before him. His heart raged in his body; a feeling of wanting to go home washed over him as he tried to weigh the decision. And in a brief moment of uncertainty, he put his hand on the first cup he felt was right. The ram smiled widely as he pulled it away. When Allen saw the rocks, his heart sank to his belly.

"How dreadfully terrifying you must feel. Seems like a bad choice, wolf." The ram chuckled as he snapped his fingers. Allen tried to make a run for it, but his gatekeeper grabbed him by his neck. Amazed the ram could wrap a whole fist around his skinny throat, Allen struggled against his captor. His eyes grew wide when a stockade appeared before them, though the wolf couldn't believe it just appeared out of the air. The wolf threw his fists over the ram's body, but they were only taps to the gatekeeper.

The wolf wanted to plead out. He wanted to break free and scream to the world of the terrors happening to him right now, of what might be happening to Mike, to Rachel. He wanted to leave the walls and never see the place again.

The ram threw Allen's body into the stockade and secured him tight. Forced to stand, bent over, the gatekeeper trailed a finger down the wolf's back and grabbed his ass firmly. "They always fight, but the game is done." Allen's nose crinkled as he started to smell the ram's musk, the stench engulfing his nostrils as he struggled against the wooden restraints.

"Let me the fuck out!" he protested, but the ram didn't listen. He grabbed the wolf's pants and ripped them off.

"I at least want a good view as I tell these tales, wolf." He let the pants and boxer briefs fall to the floor as he circled the captured wolf.

Heat started to overtake the captured wolf. Allen felt the cold air breeze along his naked ass, as he stood there, helpless to the ram's advances. Tears started to drizzle down from the wolf's eyes, grey fur getting darker and matted as the waters rushed down to the white of his cheeks. He wondered what Mike would say if he saw him like this. What would Mike do? His mind thought of the basset hound standing right next to the gatekeeper, his arms crossed, his eyes judging. Allen's ears lowered as he started to hear his boyfriend's voice surround him. "I told you I'd leave you if this happened again. I can't believe you'd cheat on me." Sniveling, he worried if his relationship would hold up if he made it out alive.

"I love you, babe," he whimpered out as the ram grabbed

his ass.

"Does your boyfriend not like your slutty side, wolf? I guess you better hope he doesn't catch us, then. I'll keep your secret, if you pay attention." The ram was whispering in Allen's ears, the wolf's nose almost crumbling at the smell of the gatekeeper's musky armpits.

Allen whined thinking about Mike. He knew there was a jealous side to the basset hound who he loved. In the back of his mind, he heard his boyfriend's voice berating him for looking at other canines. "Am I not good enough?" He always hated how Mike would get angry when he got friendly with a cashier or a waiter. He knew if Mike saw him like this, his lover would vanish. His relationship would be over. Defeated, he simply nodded at the proposition put before him. Licking the wolf's cheek, the ram drove a hard slap to Allen's ass. "Now, where do we begin?" said the ram as he took a seat before the bound wolf. A small grin swept through his face. "Oh I know. Where the blood begins to splatter," he said, placing his hand on Allen's head. The wolf felt himself lose consciousness as his eyes went pale. His body went limp, and the ram's laughter echoed in the stadium around the pair.

TOOTHACHE

PULL IT OUT
PULL IT OUT
PULL IT OUT

Barry's mind raced with voices as his mouth throbbed against his skull. The Pitbull had been plagued with toothaches in the past, but the large, muscled canine knew this one was different. He had never heard voices before, never heard anything screaming to remove a piece of himself. His vision blurred as he stood in front of his mirror, the white lights echoing the harsh magenta of his fur. He rubbed his hands over the black circles on his eyes, trying to massage the pain away. The throbbing was crippling; he leaned over his bathroom sink, shivering as each throb punched his skull over and over. Barry tried to think on what to do, all the while forgetting he was in the middle of being rimmed.

The neighbors were slamming their feet on the top floor again, but Barry tried to pay it little mind as he opened the mirror to find something to sooth his pain. A single aspirin lay on the shelf inside. The Pitbull rolled his eyes as he saw it, grabbing the pill and swallowing it quickly.

As the pain eased and allowed him back to the moment, he felt the soft tongue run along his hole, his legs quivering as the toothache died down. *This shit needs to go away,* Barry thought to himself. *Fuck knows dentists are expensive, and I barely have a dollar to give them bastards anything.* His mind started to overfill with thoughts on how to move past all that was happening. He had been plagued with the pain for a couple of days, but his body made him feel as if the pain had always been there. His brain immediately knew when the tooth would start to act up. It was instinct, a small feeling that rushed from his belly to his jaw as if the warning bells would be enough to prepare him for the throbbing rage that ensued each time it happened.

He looked behind him to find a tiger companion buried deep against his ass. He stared at the gold fur and black stripes moving slowly. His eyes stayed at the collar, then trailed down the rope it was attached to. He felt its rough material brush against his legs as he tugged at the base of the sink. Barry let out a brief sigh as he tried to return to the moment, remembering he had someone tied to the sink of his bathroom. Leaning hard against it, Barry was thankful for the relief. He felt the rope move as the tiger worked through his hole. His ass felt the softness of the blindfold he had tied around the tiger's head. As the ache died down, he relaxed his muscles and tried to enjoy the thorough work of his sexual adventure.

The tiger's hands moved along his legs, rubbing over Barry's balls. It didn't take much to get the canine hard again. A simple light touch to his shaft and he was ready to pound any bottom that willingly approached him. Barry smoothed his hands over his face and down his chest, feeling as if all was clear now. His body relaxed against the bathroom sink. *Fuck,* he thought, *I almost forgot what this feels like. Being touched. Being rimmed. It's been so long, I could just blow right here.*

His mind wandered into a flurry of memories for a quick minute. Pictures of his ex-boyfriend popped up as he closed his eyes. Barry could feel his muscles tense as he saw them float away into darkness. Barry could feel his heart yearn for what once was, but the rest of his body desired something there. Something then. He relaxed himself again as he put his mind back into the encounter.

Barry's eyes traced along his abdomen, hands gripping the sink as he relished the work his fuck toy was putting in. His eyes landed on his face, a faint smile treading across as he grew wholly relaxed.

"That's right; it has been so long, hasn't it," the reflection in the mirror uttered back to him. As he watched its lips move, the smile faded away and a surge of anxiety rushed through his blood.

It's probably the aftereffects of the toothache. Bastards do cause trouble, he thought to himself as he closed his eyes. His image made him unsettled now, his mind forcing him to see things that couldn't be real.

"Don't blow just yet, Barry. Wouldn't want your plaything to think you can't handle a simple rim job. I bet he's waiting to ride that dick soon," his reflection spoke again, his voice louder as his eyes remained closed.

"What do you want?" the Pitbull spoke aloud. His arms crossed over his chest, the fuchsia fur glowing under the dimly lit bathroom.

"What was that?" The tiger pulled away from Barry's ass. The Pitbull looked back at his fuck boy, seeing his head move around. He loved it when they couldn't see. Barry smiled as he watched for a few seconds as the tiger moved his head back and around the room.

"Nothing," Barry said as he turned around. "I thought I

heard something." The tiger didn't think much more on it, sliding his tongue along Barry's ass.

The Pitbull moved his body around to face his bound bitch. He stretched his neck to the side as he lowered his jockstrap, ready to feed his urge to facefuck his slut. He rested his cock on the tiger's face. Should have been muskier tonight; the Pitbull's mind filled with a small bit of disappointment. His tiger fuck toy brushed his hands over Barry's thick member as he rested. He let out a small moan as he inhaled every bit of musk that hit his nostrils. "Did you just bring me here for a bit of oral, sir?" he asked as he toyed with the Pitbull's cock.

Barry smirked and placed his hand on the boy's head. "I brought you here to be my personal urinal, bitch." Without pause, he started to release a stream of piss on his fuck toy. The tiger eagerly opened his mouth, swallowing what warm drops hit it. Barry moved his cock around, drenching what he could of the tiger's body, his face, his chest; Barry wanted to see the toy's fur wet with his piss. As he felt himself nearing the end of his stream, he thrust his cock into his toy's mouth, and without waiting for the Pitbull, the toy started to slide his mouth along the thick shaft that was forced inside him. Barry grunted the moment his felt his dick reach down the throat of the bitch before him. *Fuck*, he yelled to himself as he grabbed onto the sink behind him.

"He probably doesn't think you're big enough, Barry." The voice returned.

What the fuck?! He thought to himself. The Pitbull looked away from his tiger partner, and wondered what voices were sliding into his skull.

"You've never been that thick, Barry. And let's be honest, it couldn't stay up if it tried. It's so pathetic!"

Stop it! Stop it! Stop it! Worried now, Barry placed his hands over his ears and pushed down tightly.

"Fuck you! You're lucky to even get a guy back to your

place. Especially with a broke tooth like this one!" Barry's jaw throbbed again. The nerve raged inside of his skull, causing the Pitbull to take in a large breath.

Keep composure. Don't let it get it to you. The pain will go away soon, Barry told himself as the tooth continued to throb. He rubbed his cheek, hoping the massage would sooth it, pleading mentally for it to go away. The tiger picked up the pace as he felt Barry shift against the bathroom sink, using his hand to stroke the Pitbull off. The hand slid along his drenched dick. Barry let out a small moan, as if to say he loved it, though masking the agony he was sitting through.

"If it hurts you so fuckin' much, why don't you pull it out!"

PULL IT OUT
PULL IT OUT
PULL IT OUT

The words raged against this skull. Barry was having trouble staying in the moment between the words shouting at him, the pain throbbing. He couldn't keep his eyes focused on anything. The bathroom was a wash of greys and whites blending with the tiger's stripes. He pushed his partner back.

"Yo, dude, what the fuck. You alright? Did I do something?" The tiger's rope shook as he pulled away. Barry's eyes darted to the tiger as he tried to stand, only to tumble back to the floor. The Pitbull threw himself down to the ceramic tile, pained moans wailing from his mouth. The words still screaming at him.

Fine. Fine. FINE! He thought as he forced his hand against his mouth, fingers reaching in to find his back tooth. The Pitbull latched on after taking moments to get a grip.

Already loose, he forced his hand down to yank it from his jaw. The first time was unsuccessful; it made the pain worse, the throbbing growing stronger. He continued to yank and pull at the slippery bone in his mouth until he could feel wedge from his gums.

The tiger listened, confused for a moment. His arms stretched outward, trying to feel for the Pitbull writhing in pain, yet only finding air. His hands trailed along the floor, fingers slipping through blood Barry splattered. Curious, the tiger brought his fingers to his muzzle, inhaling the substance. When its metallic stench filled his nose, the tiger jumped back. "Yo, I didn't sign up for this. Let me the fuck out of here!" he yelled while Barry continued to pull his tooth from his jaw.

"You see that? Even your fuckboy wants to leave. He must think you're fuckin' crazy now, Barry."

"Shut up!" he shouted. Alone now, he focused on yanking the throbbing beast out of his body.

"Don't tell me to shut up! Just let me the fuck out of this thing!" the tiger responded, ripping the blindfold from his eyes. The moment his vision returned, his throat erupted in a raging scream. "Jesus fucking Christ!" Frantic, the tiger tried to yank the rope from the sink, bits of orange fur flying off his body as he did anything to escape without luck. He inched his body as far away from Barry as possible, afraid of getting hurt in the madness. "Stay the fuck away from me!" he yelled at the Pitbull, his body quaking fiercely as Barry tortured himself.

"You'll never get it out, Barry! It's a part of you. It's a part of one of the many things that are wrong with you!"

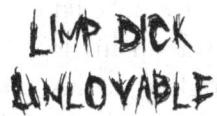

LIMP DICK
UNLOVABLE

UNFUCKABLE

PULL IT OUT
PULL IT OUT

Frustrated, Barry shot up from the ground and rammed his head against the sink. The tiger screamed wildly as he watched the Pitbull unravel. Barry flailed about, bashing himself into anything and everything he could. Blood splattered against the walls, his bathroom mirror, his sink. "Fuck!" he screamed as he continued to abuse himself, trying to get this one piece out of his body. "I just need this to go! I need it go away, I don't care where, I want it out! I want it fixed! I want to be fixed!" The Pitbull ran like a battering ram, forcing his head hard against the walls of his bathroom. Barry screamed as he felt the bones in his nose crumble on impact.

He ran to the doorway of his bathroom, falling over the tiger. "Fuck!" his companion shouted as he saw Barry raise his head. The Pitbull flung his nose around, his eye loose and flailing with each movement. He rammed his head against his dresser, the corner penetrating his cheek, blood splattering upon each impact.

"Now your eye's fucked up, Barry! How're you gonna fix that? Can't fix a broken eyeball, Barry!!"

"Shut the fuck up!" the Pitbull screamed again, driving his fingers around his eye and ripping it out. Barry raised his fist holding the eye and threw it hard into the bathroom. The eyeball bounced against the sink, then flew into the bound tiger's lap. Barry's fucktoy looked down, holding his stomach as he realized what was in his lap. His stomach couldn't handle the sight. Gurgling up his chest, the tiger spewed vomit on the floor. Bile was dripping from his mouth as he tried to escape, sliding on the pile of puke that left his body. Barry's body was a mass of pain and panic; an incendiary pile of flesh doing damage only to himself. Unable to see much, Barry got up from the floor and ran down his hall into the living room.

"You're irrational, Barry. You didn't need to yank it out like that. Now who'll love you? So much of you is missing now."

The voice continued to pummel him as he ran naked from his apartment. He made it down the first flight of stairs fine, but the moment he turned, his foot missed a step. Barry's body tumbled down the remaining set of stairs, bones crunching and penetrating his flesh. Blood spewed from his body as his neck broke on the final few steps. As he hit the last step, he watched as a tooth flew from his jaw and landed on the floor in front of him. His vision starting to blur, he couldn't see much of anything; the world faded around him as his breath came to a slow stop, a throbbing still raging against his skull.

DEATH WISH

I thought I wanted a sub. I should have checked his Mur account first, but you don't always make the best decisions when you're prowling with a hard cock against your thighs. The night was warm when I got his message. It's unusual for prey to come to me, but I opened it, assuming it wouldn't go anywhere. Hook-up apps aren't as active as one would imagine. Like a role-playing game, they're mostly stats based, and if you fit the mold, you'll get a hit. If not, silence.

SluttySkunkBoi sent me a tap, then the message. "Hey Daddy, lookin' 2 suk. U host?" He didn't have a profile picture. I always hated that. Hated this blank, greyed out circle sending me a message, hiding behind a thinly veiled cyber wall, only to have it shattered upon meet up. I had decided to ignore it when he sent his picture. His name wasn't wrong. Silver covered his skin tight body. His fur showed underneath whatever lights he used for his image. Like a silver pipe, he posed on his knees, a cock resting on his face. His hands were bound and he wore these tight purple briefs with white trim. Underneath the balls of the unknown guy resting on him, I could see his red eyes. All embers, low burning enough, yet strong to pierce through my screen. I was hooked in that moment. My cock hard, my gut said I needed this. I wanted to grab him by his thick tail and use him every which way I could. So I went for it.

"I'm down. You got any limits?" I asked him. Waiting for a reply, I started to picture my own cock ramming into his mouth. He could be my little urinal tonight.

"As long as you don't kill me, I can do just about anything x3"

"No promises!!" I replied back, then sent him the address. While I waited for him to arrive, I went to my bathroom and started to brush through my fur. I was due for a trim, but I sometimes enjoyed the look of a furrier wolf. Or as some would put it, fluffier. I combed down to my belly, a slight pudge, but nothing I thought of getting rid of. Strands of gold fur flew from my body like smoke from a frying pan. It consumed my bathroom as I straightened out my tangles. I threw on my purple and black body harness. I hated how hard it was to push my balls through the cock ring, but some pain was necessary for a good time, and aesthetically it was pleasing.

After preparing myself, I wandered back into the bedroom and started to lay out the set of toys for the evening. There were the usual dildos and gags that any good dom would have, then the restraints, and then the knives. The boy had no clue what he was going to walk into.

It wasn't long, or at least time passed quickly as I prepped for his visit. As soon as I had finished forcing my body into the harness, he knocked at the door. It was odd how coincidental it was, but I shuffled quickly to open it. The knocks were spaced out, as if a church bell ringing against my home, but no notes singing from its girthy shape. The door flushed open and he was there, the silver fem, dolled up, yet leaving nothing to the imagination. His tight shorts exposed his bulge, his shirt covered barely anything of his chest, and that tail. Fuck! That tail hovered close behind him, almost thicker than his ass.

What stars aligned to bring him to my doorstep? Whatever the universe was doing right then, I couldn't complain. A hot piece of ass just walked up to my door and said "anything daddy likes," and I was gonna enjoy every moment of that. His eyes looked me over as he passed through my door; a hand trailed along my chest. It had been awhile since anyone had played with my fur as he did. It moved slowly along my belly, then grabbed my bulge. "Not bad," he said as if verifying assumptions made before arrival. A small smile traveled across his face as he spoke again. "What's Daddy in the mood for?"

A smirk traveled across my face as I grabbed him by the head and pulled him to the floor. "You said you was lookin' to suck; why waste time talkin' when you could put your mouth to better use?"

He lowered my briefs and started to stroke my cock, his tongue gliding along the tip before he spoke again. "Aww, the puppy thinks he's a tough dom."

I smacked him quick, then pushed his mouth down my shaft and held him there. I had never had a submissive tease me before. He was confident. Cocky. But he was also prey. I could feel his tongue move along my shaft as I held him down. I thought by now he would need to glide off, but he remained at the base as if taking a thick cock was child's play to him. I pushed him off when I got tired of the smugness of his face.

The skunk inhaled a large breath, then started to stroke me again. "Not the biggest I've taken, but still not bad. You gonna get rougher, Daddy? I'd hate for you to be a boring time." He kissed my cock the moment the last letter left his lips. As if leading me into my own home, the boy started to crawl along the floor, his ass swaying underneath the gargantuan tail attached to him.

He was starting to piss me off. I was ready to murder the plump bottom crawling before me, the sight of his wiggling ass causing me to roll my eyes as I knew he'd aggravate me further. I shut the door behind us as we entered the bedroom. The boy hopped onto the bed and immediately I snatched him by his hair and yanked him to the floor. My foot pressed firmly against his cock and balls, squeezing just enough for it to hurt. "I didn't tell you to get up there, bitch." Before he could say anything further, I grabbed his mouth and squeezed it open. The tip of my cock pushed in and I started to piss inside him.

The boy slid his head down the length of my shaft, grabbing my hips and pushing me against his muzzle. Not a drop spilled as he moved along my cock, and I took the hint. When I finished I pushed him off my cock and pushed his face down into the carpet. My hand trailed down his back to the waist of his shorts, and I yanked them down. As I grabbed his balls, he let out a small moan. I pulled them through his legs, wishing I had a humbler ready, but my hands would do fine. I drove my fist into his balls, and he let out a loud yelp. "Is that all you got, Daddy?" he asked and I hit him harder. I repeated and he kept yelling louder, moans mixing with pained screams. I did this for what felt like forever, yet he was ready for more.

I grabbed a knife from the table. I didn't want to use it this early in the game, but I sliced off his clothing then kicked his ass to the middle of the room. His taunts were starting to piss me off, and instead of drawing out the night, I just wanted to get the kill over with. I grabbed the boy by his head and thrust my cock inside his ass. My knife brushed down his body, piercing his side as I fucked him.

Skunk boy let out a hard moan, spilling another taunt from his lips. "Finally," the words came down from his tongue.

I twisted the knife inside him, blood oozing from the wound, yet he only moaned harder.

"Shut the fuck up, bitch, before I gut you!" I growled in his ear as I pulled out the knife and drove it into another spot on his side.

"I'd like to see you try, Daddy," he was quick to respond. It wasn't often I found a masochist. "You'll be lucky if I let you finish," he added as he bashed his head against mine. I fell backwards from the impact, pulling out, yet leaving the knife in his body. Before I could get up, I watched him pull it out.

I started to crawl away from him, but he grabbed my foot and brought it to his chest. I kicked up at him to try and break free, but he sliced the attacking paw. Still struggling, he held my foot to his chest and started to carve at the ankle. I could feel the blade glide through my flesh and wrap around my ankle. I screamed as I felt his claws push inside the wound and start tugging the flesh down toward him. It was a slow process, me writhing on the ground as he sliced and clawed to get the insides of my foot showing.

"What the fuck are you doing!" I screamed, trying to kick at him again, my flesh plopping to the ground of my bedroom. He dropped my foot and I tried to crawl away. My only goal was to escape. What I thought would be a good kill was not how I imagined it. I inched my way to the bedroom door, but before I could reach its stained, rough wood, I felt a hand grab my arms, restraints binding them tight.

"You can't leave yet, sir. I've not had any fun tonight. You've been a rather boring host," he said as he grabbed my ass and spread my cheeks wide. "I made this dildo myself, and by made, I mean I just wrapped a good length of barbed wire. It's fun hearing the screams that come from this." I couldn't see anything he was doing behind me. I felt a cold dampness and fingers rubbing along my hole. I felt them slide in down to the knuckle. His fingers spread apart inside me, my cock hard from the treatment. My body quivered underneath his teasing, yet I was mortified at myself. How could I let myself get caught like this? His fingers slid out from me, then I felt something metallic enter. The cold tool started spreading my hole wide. I grunted, trying to shake anything in my body out, yet it was of no use. Once he stopped spreading my ass, I felt the toy. He teased it at first, scraping the edges of my ass. I continued to grunt, pain spreading throughout my body, dread heavy in my chest. He pushed it in, the wire tearing apart whatever it latched onto inside me, his arm jolting with each shove. I screamed wildly, feeling each inch tear me apart inside. I couldn't bear the scraping and slicing he was doing to me. My hole oozed with blood. I could feel it inch along my body as he continued to twist the sharp object into me. I wanted nothing more than for it to leave me, to exit my body, but he wasn't about to take it out. And like that, the toy was shoved into my hole. My breathing quickened as I tried to push all of the pain out of my mind. I needed to focus on escaping, not the torture he was putting me through.

"Fuck fuck fuck!!" I screamed out. "You fucking fuck!" I couldn't say anything else. I needed every bit of pain to stop. My foot still hadn't numbed, my ass throbbing. What more could this boy do? What more could he want? I was starting to lose.

"Your eyes are close to begging me to kill you," he teased as he rolled me over. His hand wore a glove with claws sharpened at the edges. "We skunks have to improvise if we want claws as sharp as cats." He took them and sliced them all down my torso. Blood poured out from my body. My heart could almost jump through the cuts he made. I tried kicking up my good leg, but he just clawed it to hell. I kept kicking and kicking until I got a good shot against his face. When he pushed back I tried to make a run for it, crawling furiously, though barely making progress without my hands.

He jumped at me, grabbing my head, dragging me across and into the wall hard.

"Why are you doing this?" I said desperately. Though it was ironic, we all have a desire to know why.

"You don't need a reason to kill, sir. You just have to fucking do it." He pushed my back against the wall and licked my face. His body slid down and started to tease my cock. And in its usual nature, it propped right up the moment it's touched, ignoring all the pain surging through my body. Positioning himself, he started to ride me, a slow pulsing beat. Shaking, I let out an awkward moan, a moan filled with gargled agony as he worked along my shaft. "Daddy like that?" he asked, taking his glove and sliding his claws along my cheek. Another moan left my mouth as he held my down. My heart surged as I felt his claw move along my cheek, moving upward, slicing randomly as if I were a canvas and he was the painter. Before I could try to fight back his claw drove right into my eye. I screamed wildly as he rode my cock faster. Giggling, I could feel his ass squeeze along my shaft as he ripped my eye out from the socket.

"S-Stop! N-No m-m-more!" I tried to say. He just laughed as he rode me harder. I could feel my climax nearing its peak. My cock felt as if it were ready to burst open.

"Cum for me, Daddy," he said as he sliced down my chest with his claws. His grey fur was almost covered in my blood. He was an entirely different skunk than when he arrived. Hot, yet destructive. Not the meek boy that was eager to fuck, but a boy eager to murder.

He then trailed the metal knives at the edge of his glove down my cheek, slicing my face some more. Haunted moans left my throat as I felt myself blow, my cock shooting my load into him. Whatever I was experiencing between suffering and pleasure, I couldn't define.

"Guess I better clean it up, huh, sir?" the boy asked,

sliding off my cock and positioning his ass against my muzzle. His mouth wrapped around my wet cock, gliding along it. I tried to knock him off, but in my weakened state, I could do nothing. I felt his knives along my thighs and I grunted harder.

A light giggle came from him. They dug into my leg as he started to spray my face. I had never before been soaked by whatever stink came from a skunk's ass, but I knew I'd never want it to happen again if I lived through this. "Give your boy a little love, Daddy. I have earned it tonight, wouldn't you say?" I didn't want to lick his ass, I didn't want to open my mouth, but as soon as I felt a knife against my cock, I was quick to lick all inside him. I dug my tongue deep to keep my dick safe. I worked every inch of his hole and he continued to suck me off, teasing the tip of my cock. I squirmed underneath him, my body waiting for all of this to be over. He had me lost in the moment, constantly pushed and pulled between the pain and his teasing. Before I could blow another load into his mouth, I howled in agony. The boy sliced off my cock. I felt his knifes snip through and I heard it plop to the floor.

"You won't be needing that anymore, Sir," he said, pulling away from me. I watched him take his phone out and snap a picture, the little fake shutter sound booming in the room. He walked up to me and toyed with my throat for a moment, claws tickling my fur. I wanted to say something, anything, but before my lips could form words, he shoved his sharp fingers into my mouth, my tongue sliced up as he pushed them down to my throat. I tried to bite down, my body weak from torture. My teeth couldn't penetrate his glove. My jaw was a weak and tattered part of me, wrecked like the rest of my body. I could only taste blood as it flooded my muzzle. His fingers wriggled in the tight space as my throat was cut all inside. He twisted the objects around, turning his wrist as far as he was able to. The skunk sighed, his grey fur turning dark red from his time here. The boy pulled out and held the claws against my throat, slicing across. "At least you'll make a good selfie. Your fur is perfect for all this blood," he said as he took his phone and posed us both, my eyes dull as I saw us on his screen. He held up two fingers and stuck his tongue out. I lay behind him, propped against the wall. What a way to die, seeing yourself broken before life leaves your body. I reached out as he snapped his photos, but my arm fell short. I watched the flash go off two-three-four times before the world around me went black.

THE JUNKMAN

The cold stabbed his fur as he walked out from the airport. Gordy cursed the venture into new territory, setting his bags down and scanning for his ride, yet finding only an empty roadway. He patted down his pockets, trying to find a pack of cigarettes, yet only finding loose change and crumpled receipts from meals he had during layovers.

His body craved the taste of tar and ash—craved the act of taking a small stick and setting it between his lips. The image of smoke filling his lungs as he let out a large sigh became an all too repeating fantasy for him as he started to regret his decision to quit more and more. Yanking his phone out of his jacket pocket, he swiped it on and sent a text. "I'm here. Goddamn it's fuckin' freezing out here."

"Almost there, baby. Can't wait to finally see you in the flesh <3" he read back to himself. The message warmed him a little, but it did nothing to keep him from quaking in the dark northern cold. His hands shuffled furiously as he put his phone in his pocket, then ruffled them through his short black hair. His antlers hung high over his head, something he'd always been proud of. To most deer, the larger the antlers, the larger the cock.

He waited in the cold with a patience unknown to him before. Not one to enjoy freezing, he stood under the flickering airport lights, the glowing nature of his red fur coming out every time the lights shut off. He was a blend of red and white; could be seen easily in the dark. His golden eyes stared down the pathway and saw a car approaching. It wasn't expensive; a beat-up sedan for the modest person living anywhere in the country, its dark grey exterior shown dull under the piss poor airport lighting. He couldn't hear the car as it neared him, a plane taking off in the background as he stared right into the headlights.

He quickly latched onto his gym bag and stood at the edge of the sidewalk, but feared it made him look too eager, yet at the same time he was really anxious to get in the car. Fears of being catfished bubbled along his arms, giving him tiny goosebumps as he couldn't see the driver from the distance.

His eyes glared in the headlights as the car settled in front of him. A smile wide as his face spread like cracks in the earth as he stared at his lover through the windshield. Everything matched; the sky blue of the coyote's fur, ashes in his eyes, the snow on his chest. Every picture, every chatlog, everything matched. "Perfection." The word left his lips as he meandered to the car and opened the backseat to toss his luggage. He hopped into the passenger seat, rubbed his hands to get warm, keeping himself from attacking his lover with first time kisses and stranglehold hugs. "Ash, oh my god," was all he said, staring at the pale blue coyote in the driver's seat. A wave of emotions flooded him. It was as if his brain short circuited, not able to say any more than he just spoke. Flurries of excitement and relief fused with him.

Ash put his hand on Gordy's cheek and pulled him in for a kiss, a small slip of tongue pushing past Gordy's lips. Before Ash could pull away, Gordy pushed in for a second kiss; he had been longing for too long and needed more to quench his fix. He savored every single moment, their breaths hard and heavy as Gordy placed his hand on his lover's face, pushing away strands of his hair. Strands of fur danced in the air like cigarette smoke; a lingering gift to the air as they could not keep themselves apart. Their lips battled each other until suddenly the car behind them screamed, their horn bleeding out like a gutted pig in the cold, northern night.

Broken apart at last, Ash smiled and put the car in drive, speeding off. Gordy rolled the window down and flipped off the car behind them as if to say, "don't ever fucking bother us like that again." A passive aggressive gesture.

"How was your flight?" Ash asked as he fiddled with the GPS on his phone.

Gordy stretched his neck, ears flattening in the process as he curved it to one side, rolling it back and then curving it to the other side, letting out a large sigh. "Shitty, but everything's better now that I'm with you," he said with a wink. Ash shook his head and let out a small chuckle.

"You never said you were cheesy," he responded.

"You never said you were a cute coyote, but here we are." Gordy put his hand on Ash's as they drove through the blackened streets. "So how eager were you to see me, finally?" he followed, trying to drown out the silence and the car's worrisome squealing.

Ash placed a hand on Gordy's thigh and gripped firmly in response. His thin hands seemed fragile to Gordy, as if he could pull ash's hand by a finger, and it would plop off like an apple from a tree. His eyes traveled slowly up his partner's arm, a finger following swiftly behind. Gordy let out a heavy sigh as he took in the feel of Ash's smooth fur on his, a small sensation he had wanted more than a cigarette since he landed.

As the car pulled into the driveway of Ash's home, a

slow jazz oozed from the speakers. Gordy hummed low to the rhythm, moving in to kiss Ash before he could shut off the car. A quick peck, as Gordy sung low, *"I gave my heart to you, the one that I trusted—"* A second peck, their breath connecting as his tongue slid inside then retracted swiftly— *"You brought it back to me all broken and busted."* He let a small chuckle escape his lips as Ash finally shut off the car. He didn't want to move away, heads connecting; he wanted to stay in the moment, but the cold winter seeped through. "I didn't take you for someone who liked jazz," Gordy said as Ash opened the car door.

Ash put his hand on Gordy's cheek and smiled softly. "I don't. Spotify must have messed up on me. But now I know you do."

They walked up the steps into the house. Gordy's breath wafted in the air like smoke as he waited for Ash to unlock the door. His eyes fumbled around, the dark of the porch overtaking him. "So, are you the junkman?" Gordy asked as they entered inside, the warmth of the house hitting his face as quickly as a strong glass of whisky. Ash looked at him with confusion, not understanding the question, and Gordy smiled. "You're cuter than I expected. It's from the song; Washington sings of how she sold her heart to this junkman. He broke her heart, and she'll never love again."

Ash started to hum the song as he shed his shirt, his tail swirling to the beat as he moved into Gordy's arms. His hands brushed through the deer's short red fur, trailing down and grabbing onto his lover's jacket. Pushing it off, he swayed as if the music were still playing in the background, then leaned in and nibbled on Gordy's ear. "I guess you'll have to find out," he responded in a whisper, pulling the man into his room. In a fit of mania, Gordy pushed his lips onto Ash's, his hands grabbing his partner's ass. Gordy had been waiting for that for months, talking about it online, sending dick pics and nudes between each other. He'd wanted that man more than anything, and there, in the first few moments, he got it.

Ash's hands moved down towards Gordy's crotch, unzipping his jeans and sliding his hand inside. The seductive coyote teased his partner's cock, waking it up as he pushed him onto the bed. Gordy let out a mild grunt as Ash pulled away from him, sliding his pants down. His hand latched onto Gordy's throbbing member as he slid his tongue across the tip. His mouth worked hungrily along his partner's stiff shaft. Gordy's hand ran through Ash's hair, his fingers trailing through each strand he could grab before thrusting him down onto the full length of his dick. "Goddamn." The word escaped his lips as if it were his first time.

Ash pushed off and climbed onto the bed. His tongue traveled across Gordy's stomach, moving up along his chest and the curve of his neck. He landed right on Gordy's lips as he lowered his ass onto his lover's cock, using what saliva was left. A blend of blue and red danced together on the mattress. Gordy's antlers rocked against the walls as his partner pushed himself down to his base. The coyote's moans collided with his partner's grunts as he rode him hard.

Gordy took his hands and moved the fiery fingers along his lover's back, grabbing tight as if the moment would trail off in a ball of confusion, leaving only his imagination running through the clouds. The lights never dimmed, fluorescent brightness hanging over them in the beige white of the room. Every time he opened his eyes, Gordy thought of how that perfect sky blue clashed so hard with those meager beige walls. Ash was the best feature there; the rest could bleed away.

There was a part of Gordy that couldn't believe that was happening, that it was real. His fingers grabbed onto Ash's fur more tightly. In a fit of mania, he pushed Ash onto his back, his tongue sliding along the curve of his lover's neck. Gordy rammed himself in hard, his hips pounding at a furious pace.

Gordy's hands pressed hard against Ash's shoulders, yet something odd happened beneath them. His eyes closed, he could feel his fingers slide, as if he were holding onto mush. His tongue lashed as his mouth sucked hard against Ash's neck, and soon blood seeped between his lips. Confused, Gordy opened his eyes to see if he bit his partner, yet before he could ascertain any damage, his cock started to tingle inside Ash's ass.

"I was hoping you'd be an asshole. It'd make this easier on me," he heard Ash say, and before he could respond, a sharp pain shot through his groin and up his hips. It was as if lightning struck the tip of his cock and it reached so far inside his body, his skull would explode.

His mind was a blizzard of thoughts; mixtures of pain and confusion rattled around his head. His eyes blurred his vision. He placed a hand onto Ash's chest to push away from his lover's body. He could feel it sink into the flesh, and as his vision steadied, he could see Ash's face contorting, spreading wide. Ash was a slowly becoming a plot of clay, fur and flesh spreading and tearing apart. "I guess the junkman got you tonight." His voice was distorted as Gordy finally got away. He fell off the bed and against the wall. He stared at his crotch, only to find his cock missing.

"What the fuck? Did your ass just..." Gordy shouted in confusion. "Where the fuck is my dick?" he shouted again. Ash said nothing as his body changed, his body tearing apart at his chest, teeth exposing themselves underneath. Gordy took the first thing he could grab, his shoe, and threw it at the monster before him, yet it was torn apart. He pushed himself up and tried to run for the door, yet Ash caught him, tearing Gordy's back hart with his claws. Gordy kicked back, only to have his foot bitten off in Ash's chest.

"I'm all teeth on the inside, Gordy. And fuck Christ am I

hungry," Ash responded, pulling his victim close.

"What the fuck, man. What fucked up thing are you?" Gordy shouted, and Ash started to devour the rest of his leg. Gordy screamed wilder than a banshee. The pain of being eaten at this slow rate was too much for him to handle. His blood splattered all over the creature's body as he was munched on. He could taste his own blood ooze from his throat. Gordy grew weaker, his body shutting down as he heard the monster crunching on his bones. The world around him growing distant, he wasn't able to fight any longer. In his last fit of consciousness, he grabbed his cellphone, only to pass out before he could call for help.

The beast took all of Gordy's lower half before he finally emitted his final breath. Ash's body crunched every shattered bone like a woodchipper, the blood and flesh sliding down the monster's insides. It wasn't satiated until Ash had every limb and piece of his former lover. Within a matter of moments, Gordy was devoured, and Ash, though satiated, started searching for another victim.

INTERLUDE 2

ABSCONDENCE

Mike didn't know what to expect as he ventured further down the hall. His gut raging with each step he took, Mike tried to calm himself and regain his courage. The basset hound rubbed his paws through his muzzle, his cheeks stretched with the massage of his fingers. He watched as bits of brown and white fur shed from his body; he knew panic was filling up inside him. Mike wondered how long he'd be able to keep himself calm before he blew up. Before he freaked out. At first glance the walls remained the same. He began to loathe the dank purple wallpaper the more he saw it. He also began to loathe the silence of his guide.

"So, how long you been doing this?" he asked nervously. He needed something to take his mind over how monotonous the hall was. But the guide didn't answer. "Not much of a talker, are you?" He asked a different question, hoping the passive aggression would sink in to his guide and force him to speak up. But still the guide didn't answer.

Mike gave up trying to talk to the guide, but he did

glance over to see if the guide was even there. He cursed the long robes worn by them, hoping to at least see some ass, but the universe was not in his favor that evening. The end of the hall was coming up. "Oh, are we finished already?" he asked teasingly. The guide stopped and turned around to look at the basset hound. Its glowing eyes studied the brown and white splotches of Mike's fur, and the chubbiness of his belly. The guide shook its head no, then pointed down to a door waiting at the end. Above, the door had an inscription. Mike shrugged and ran towards it, shortly standing before a tall wooden door curving at the top. He saw the handle was made of gold. He touched the inscription on it, reading it out loud. "No tales safe for living souls lie beyond this door." He read it again and started to laugh. "It can't be that bad!" he said as he pushed open the door and crossed the threshold.

The moment his foot stepped into the new part of the house, everything changed. He could see creatures wandering around as if lost. He noticed they looked like frogs, lizards, and turtles. Their faces were full of scales, eyes bulging, some with shells and others with spikes driven from their skulls. They were all grey, as if someone had taken the color out of every creature there.

Fear started to creep into his body the further he moved into the hall. Everyone was battered. Everyone was solemn. Everyone was lost. He grabbed one of the creatures and held its shoulders. "What the fuck is this?" he asked and the creature rubbed its scaly paw along his hand.

"We are all wanderers here. Though we had purpose at one time, we've all gotten lost, unable to find our way to the exit. Unable to escape." It stared at him. Mike thought of how empty that face was. He couldn't feel anything other than horror as he continued to stare into the eyes of the creature.

"How does one get out of this hall?" he asked and the frog-like creature pointed him inward.

"Follow the path. Don't stray from it, no matter what comes your way," it said then pushed away. It wandered into a sea of creatures.

Mike saw no other option and started to wander down the path. He looked around and noticed how desolate it was there. It was as if he entered a cave. The floor of the home had turned into dirt and gravel; the walls were stone; some of the monsters lingering around had started fires while others stared at nothing. As he moved forward, he noticed a small few slamming their heads against the stone.

The cave was filled with moans. Although most did nothing, there were a small few who were crying at the edges of the path. The atmosphere, the cries, the banging of flesh against stone, all were noises that began to terrorize his ears. He was starting to go mad by the constant noise, each moment inside growing louder and louder. Mike started to run, doing anything he could to just make it through to the end of his journey. His steps got faster as more of the creatures started to appear. Panic was setting in his chest. His eyes widened the further he got in.

"What the fuck is happening?" he said aloud as he ran. He ran faster than he ever had before. He looked behind him and the creatures were all running away, running with him. The ground started to shake. He knew something was coming, but didn't know what. He felt it. He knew it'd be huge. Mike thought of the creatures around him as a giant creature terrorizing everything in its path. He could feel it get closer as he ran further. For a brief moment, he looked back.

"What the fuck is happening?" he shouted as his feet carried him with the rest of the crowd. They were like small children in his eyes, all panicked reptilian creatures running en masse away from some impending doom; something they all felt inside like another sense. Mike ran faster than he ever had before, his feet kicking up dirt with each heavy step into the ground. He knew something was coming, felt it like everyone else there. He ran because he knew something big was behind them, and he didn't want to be the one to see it with his eyes. The basset hound had never felt this kind of fear before. He'd been afraid, but he never had to fear the day he would die. He never once imagined what it would be like if his heart stopped beating, if he stopped breathing, if the world around him just faded away from his eyes. The dread bubbling inside his belly was new for him, like bad indigestion on a taco night. His whole body ached as he ran as far away as he could, passing rocks and blackness in this cave. His eyes darted up and small winged creatures flew down from the rocky spires hanging above them. "None of this is real," he told himself. "Houses can't turn into caves, not in a split second they can't. This isn't possible." His voice grew louder, words echoing against the walls of this natural abyss he was trapped in.

"But anything is possible in Carnage, love." Mike's dread spread wide in his body as the voice made his back shudder. The fur on his body stood up, his eyes widened; Mike did everything in his power to keep moving, his legs burning with every inch forward he made.

Then he saw it. His feet stopped in the dirt as he saw a minotaur towering over him and the sea of small creatures around him. His neck arched upward to see the beast stories above him, the beast's cock dangling feet above his head. "Oh, fuck!" he yelled as his eyes trailed over the dark red fur covering the muscled creature that stood above everything in this cave. A huge blood-furred bull swung down with an arm and picked up some of the creatures that were running. He dangled the bodies he caught over his mouth and dropped them down like grapes, his teeth crunching down on their bodies and swallowing. The basset hound's stomach turned as he watched blood drip from the corners of the bull's maw as the beast turned his attention to another group and swept up what he could. Mike watched as his teeth chewed through bones and scales and flesh. He didn't know what do to but stare, his eyes trailing over the glowing red of the bull's body. He could see the horns chipped from the ground, the bull's eyes empty, only circles holding pale white inside. The beast's nose ring swung each time his jaw chomped down, its neck pulsing each time it swallowed a new batch of food. The bull's arms rubbed along its belly. Mike's eyes followed as the beast's hands grabbed its cock and started to stroke himself. Shaking violently, Mike nearly fell as the beast roared, an erupting gargle of noise attacking the rocky walls they were held in. "Fuck Christ!" he exclaimed, the minotaur swinging down and grabbing him in one raging motion. The hound looked death in the eyes as he saw the beast open his jaws. Like a claw machine, the basset hound felt the minotaur's fingers open. His throat screamed as he fell furiously, scraping his arm on the bull's teeth as he plunged into the beast's belly. Mike tried to grab onto something, his claws digging into the bull's throat as he fell downward. It slowed up, but not enough to stop him in the air. Another roar flew past his body, forcing him upward, only to have gravity pull him down again. Mike's nose was attacked every moment he was inside the carnivorous monster's mouth, the smell of rotting flesh filling his body every time he breathed in. As he went down the bull's throat, everything went black for a moment. Before he could utter another curse on the world, his eyes started to form something.

"Fuck!" Mike screamed as he felt his face hit something hard beneath him. His fingers played with the warm surface, immediately letting him know he hit asphalt. In a slow motion, he brought himself to his knees, seeing the night sky above him, lit up by burning houses. And before he could move out of the road, his fur stood from the breeze in the air. A pair of lights flashed on him, and as his eyes turned towards them, he felt everything fade around him.

DESOLATION

I packed the first bag the day things started to go downhill. The day I noticed he wasn't Riley anymore. Not the Riley I knew anyways. Together for seven years, but it was a slow decline. Or maybe it wasn't. My memory don't serve me so damn good anymore. Everybody says the seven-year itch is a bitch, but this wasn't it.

When I look back at who we've always been, it's different than living in the moment. In those moments everything was just right. We were kids, still figuring ourselves out, still waiting to take on the world because we had a lot of life left in us. But looking back, there were cracks lingering between us that I wish I had felt back then. You don't always feel it when you should. That's all a part of life, I guess. Or maybe it ain't, maybe I'm just the unlucky bastard who drew the wrong straw and took this path.

It was my birthday when I realized we were done. I said we should eat at the House of Pies, but he didn't want to. Said the food was bland; that he knew I had no taste but to pick the one restaurant because the pies was good was insufferable. I let him choose where we ate that night because ain't that what you're supposed to do? Toss away everything for yourself and ensure your lover's happiness? At least, that's what I thought was right. Or maybe I did it because I was weak. Right now things are just a blur.

It's funny, y'know, trying to look back at an entire lifespan of a relationship and see only fuzzy lines like a tube TV gone bad—like the VCR ain't clean. It's like you live those moments and as you live them they're the best fucking thing every, but then you look back and see all the red flags, the warning signs, the flashing lights that tell you to get as far away as possible, but you don't want to believe them when you're alive. Right then. All you want is for that beautiful disaster to remain whole. Forever. But even forever has cracks in it. Like a car leaking oil, the good bleeds dry.

Riley was a helluva rabbit, the whitest fucking fur you ever seen. It was like snow, just sticking to a body, ears tipped with blue that seemed unnatural. It was like the sky on a fall afternoon in Texas. Just blue, pure fucking blue, same as his eyes. When I married him, I got lost in his ocean.

Though my fur was short, that tight assed bunny knew how to make it stand on edge. The day we said our "I Do's" he rubbed his paws along my mane, the gold of my hair shivering along the navy waters of my fur. I was the happiest horse that day.

We never left each other's arms, cuddling, holding hands at dinner; we were connected by touch the whole day. It was the most contact I had in our whole relationship, and I was happy to get that morsel he tossed at me.

But that was who we were. Together, yet apart because he would get uncomfortable with touching. Even if I brushed his arm he would wince, or push me away. When we slept together in bed, I had one small coffin area I was confined to. Not able to cross the line or get in his area or he couldn't sleep.

I kept to these rules. What else are you to do when you love someone? I kept to them well.

The week after my birthday, I was changing the oil on our car. Though it was in my name, I liked to think we owned it. It was ours. Paid off, no car note, just the upkeep. He never drove, but it didn't matter. I was happy to spin around town. Driving took the edge off my shoulders. There's a peace to it all when you're zooming down the freeway, the world a blur and the music blazing through the speakers. It was always a momentary nirvana.

The sun was just above us both as he walked his limber body from the home. He wore the same clothes as he did three days ago. He swore he changed, but he never did. The same cheeto stains on his shirt glowed in the afternoon air.

He tapped me on my thigh and I just about beat my head against the car, but I pushed my body out from underneath the 5K piece of machinery and sat up staring at him. He said, "I wish you had a spine that could carry more than the weight of your gut."

The sun burned into the darkness of my fur. If there were ever a more miserable time to start a fight, right then and there was it. I busted my hands through the gold strands of my hair and looked up at him, eyes squinted. Confused. Hot. I don't always keep my cool in the worst conditions. So I just spat back, "Yea, well, I sometimes wish you weren't a tight assed bitch all the time." He didn't take that too well.

"Goddammit, JC, you're fucking pathetic, you know that? You would let the world walk all over you if you let them. And you do, you just don't want to believe it. Barely a man at all if you ask me."

"Yea, well who the fuck is asking you, anyways?" I was pissed by this point. Blood toiled underneath flesh. I took a rag from my back pocket and started wiping the oil off my hands. You could never tell if it got off, though; Navy and Oil are just too intertwined in darkness to stay visible.

He took a sip of his Mt. Dew, well, more of a chug but what do I know. I just remember his throat pulsing as the carbonated liquid slide down. Drops of green oozing down the sides of his mouth and sticking to his white fur. Upon finishing a loud burp erupted from his mouth, the stench of salt and cheetos lingering in the air. He looked me dead in the face. "I was just thinking about it. Just thinking how you're not the man I imagined marrying. Just the shell of what I wanted."

I packed more bags that night.

I had just gotten off of work. Untucked my shirt, my belly bulging a bit from being stuffed underneath the tightness of a button down and slacks that I'd worn for a few days. Normally I didn't reuse them, but the laundry wasn't done and God help asking for help.

I tossed my clothes and just meandered around the house in a pair of black briefs. Riley always hated that. If I could get away with it, I'd wander nude, but he hated the sight of a naked body on a good day. The days had been bad and I wasn't ready to see what that would look like.

He had already started on the whiskey. Full this morning, he had torn through most of the bottle as he lounged in the same clothes as yesterday, and the day before, and the day before. It was weird. The house was silent. It was as if our power went out, yet all the lights worked. There was no screaming at the game console, no clicking of the mouse or furious typing. Even his breathing was quiet.

I stepped into the living room, the dim lights enlivening the darkened blue of my fur. What night sky should I have become that night? When I think back to it, I wished I were empty. Yet my fur carried a small flurry of stars at its edges, like Atlantean tears. Pleiades escaped, I found Riley sitting in his office chair, downing a glass of Jameson. His chair squealed like a pig up for slaughter; as if our neighbor were lying in our living room waiting for him to drive the knife in his protruding belly so that he may eat of him. And when I looked into his eyes, there was nothing.

They were a metaphor for emptiness; a symbol of vacancy that was beyond any description I could muster. I just know it was cold, so goddamn cold. "I want you to fuck me." The words were as cold as the rest of him. Normally, you wouldn't have to tell me twice to stick my dick in you, but there was something different about this. Something not right. And before I could even force a syllable from my lips he started again. "I want you to rape me. Beat me. I want you to make me worthless, 'cause I am worthless. I am an impossible disaster. Just like my father always told me."

What the fuck was he asking? We had talked about getting rougher in bed before. He'd wanted light punching, and maybe finally some anal since that had been lacking for years, but what the fuck was he setting before me? I stood before him, dumbfounded. "No." It was all I could utter. I couldn't fathom anything at that moment. I couldn't bring my stars to align and say anything other than "no."

And I saw it. Every inch of glass that made his body just shatter. Riley started shaking, a tear streaming down from his face as he lifted his fist and started ramming it into his face. Over, and over, just pummeling himself. Bits of white fur flung through the air as his thin arms wailed into whatever part of his body he could manage to find.

I shot in to grab his arm, but the moment I touched him, his fist rammed right into my chest and I was thrown to the floor. He beat himself for what seemed like hours. He pummeled his belly, his balls, face, everything he could reach until he finally calmed down. Then he spoke, and whatever pain I felt in my body just intensified, as if a bad toothache flourished to my hooves. "A real man would have stopped me. But you're just a shell. A spineless being with a cock that's incompatible with my body. Why the fuck do you even love me?" He squatted down and placed his hand on my shoulder as I pulled myself up. "Somedays, I just wish you'd kill yourself."

"You know, I worry you'll leave me." he lay on my lap, his hand brushing my leg as we watched TV in the living room. His fingers teased the shortness of my dark fur then moved to connecting dots that were strung along my body. A week since he threw me to the floor, he clung to me as if I were his last chance at life. As if he needed me to keep him alive, else what would the world do to him if I were gone? But that was him, knowing exactly what buttons to push to keep me safe. To make me feel as if everything that had happened was just a one.time deal and that it'd never happen again.

I sipped my evening coffee, something he even made. Granted, he didn't get it right, but who was I to ignore the gesture? "I ain't left you yet, have I?" I said that, yet I'd been packing my bags with every incident that happened. Little by little, taking them to a storage unit, planning what escape I could while he slept. Whatever ride we were on was ending, and ending soon.

There was something bitter about this coffee. I know. All coffee is bitter, but this was different. This was powdery, as if something was mixed in but not well. I shrugged it off to just powdered creamer, but the texture seemed more aspirin than cream. It didn't take long for me to feel it. An overwhelming sense of exhaustion curling over my bones. My body sinking into the couch, muscles relaxed to the point of numb and calm. My fingers let go of my cup, coffee spilling over me and the rabbit. He jumped up and said something, but my brain couldn't quite comprehend what was going on. Slowly, everything went black.

I could tell I was dreaming. Though the sun was warm across my body, and the sand felt good on my feet, I knew my brain was bringing up desires to soothe my slumber. He lay on the beach, a pair of trunks. The waves flowed seamlessly onto the shore as we relaxed.

"I've never been to a beach before; my family always wanted to take me, but we never did. A creek? Yes, but never a beach," he said, lifting himself up.

"Well, now you have, babe. It's nice being out for once. The house was getting a little too crowded."

His eyes stared me dead. It was like I said something that set him off. "You don't like being home? You don't like that I'm there?"

"That's not it, babe. It's just nice to get out every once in a while," I quickly responded.

"Oh, yeah, I'm sure. Fuck, JC. why can't you just not say whatever's on your mind? You ruin so much just by talking."

"Fuck this, I'm out of here," I said, walking away. I wandered off into the ocean, the waves encompassing my body. I could see the sky change, but I didn't care. I wanted to be held by something, anything. And these waters welcomed me with open arms. Welcomed me because they had no one else to welcome. I sunk down into its depths, let the blues turn black.

That was not a dream that I wanted to remain in.

"I know you're leaving." The words were cold, traveling cold waters as they left his lips. Each letter was a boat that swam around my skull as I started to wake up. My body was relaxed, as if I had never gotten such a good sleep until now. The kind of sleep you have after the best sex in your life. The room a blur still, I tried to sit up, but a hand pushed me back down. I could feel our bed under me. I could feel my hands and legs bound together. The rope irritated my short blue fur. I wondered if my stars were shining, or if they disappeared during my slumber.

"What's going on?" The words were lazy. Limping off my tongue as if they were a midnight drunk wandering home. My mind started to release the anxiety through my body. I could hear my heart beating quicker, my hands struggling against the ropes as my eyes finally saw our room clearly. Dimly lit by the lamp, he stood over me, brushing the gold of my hair.

"I know you're leaving me, JC. I saw you packing your bags the other night." I struggled hard against the bindings, but nothing was loosening them.

"I was going to tell you, I just needed..."

"The right time? Fuck, there is no right time, you miserable stupid fuck! And honestly, did you think you were just going to leave? I need you, goddammit. You may be the stupidest boy in the world, but I fucking need you." His face was a concoction of fear and anger. Eyes widened, yet the ocean in his eyes looked like they were on the brink of a storm. An ugly storm. His fur looked ragged. I knew he hadn't bathed in a while, but damn, was every strand dead set on reaching the sky their own way. His ears were kept down. He was wild as he stood in front of me. The wildest person I'd ever seen. And I had nothing to defend myself, only bindings. To keep me tied down tight.

"Need me? For what? You seem so dead set on making me out to be so worthless. Why would you need someone who means nothing to you?" I don't know if that was really what I wanted to ask, but those were the words that slid out.

"I don't mean it when I call you stupid. It's a joke. I've told you this before, but no you gotta go and be all pansy about it. I love you, JC, yet you just see it as me being 'mean' to you." His arms were flailing around as if the madness were taking him over. I started to wonder if he was always this mad, always this little bit of crazy lingering in his body only to come out in the most urgent of times. I wondered if this was our decline or if he had always had this darkness in his heart. I kept working the ropes, pulling my hands apart, thinking if I could just wear them down then I could get free. I wriggled them around, yet the ropes were strong against me. "I need you; you're the only one who will love me. Who would even consider loving a monster like I am? I need you to stay." I could hear the tears slide down his cheeks. His voice started to break, a giant wail escaping his throat as he threw himself on top of me. My bare chest getting soaked in his tears. His hand moved down and grabbed my bulge, my briefs hugging me tight. His hand slowly massaged away, my cock hardening. What was happening right then? What was I going through? This madness washed over us like lava spewing from a dormant volcano. His desperation, his insanity started to control us there in this room. I had to get away. Riley was changing right in front of me, various forms of the monster bleeding from his fur. How long did it lie dormant inside him? "Please, stay. I'll do anything. I'll let you fuck me more often, see? You like that, right?"

I struggled against him, bucking his hand away. My elbow connected with his face. A sliver of night sky clashed with his face. He was no longer the blue sky I had been in love with. This monster was now different. Desperate. Cold. It was like all his fears and anger just entered into a boiling pot and they just started popping off as they heated up. He let out a harsh, shattering scream and hopped off the bed. As he assessed his face, I wriggled violently, trying to break free from the bed. I needed to get away. I needed to get out. He ran out of the room and came back with a pot, steaming. I fell to the floor in my raging escape and he poured the contents of the pot all over the back of my left legs. He burned me; I could hear my flesh boil as he poured. I couldn't keep from screaming; what resolve I carried inside me left the moment the water rushed over my limb. My voice erupted in a violence unknown to me before then.

He took the pot and shoved it hard into my back, burning what night sky I carried there. I bucked up, but he shoved me back down. When I saw my hands in front of my face, I forced my mouth on the ropes and started to gnaw hard, my throat still screaming from the pain. He left the room as my teeth chewed furiously. As I felt the rope loosen he returned, his sewing kit in hand. "I won't hurt you anymore if you say you're not leaving. I will do anything to keep the best relationship I've ever had. You're the only one who'll let me walk all over you."

He started driving his sewing needles along my shoulder blades, sending them in deep yet slow. Though the pain was minimal, he knew of my fear of needles well. He knew the slowness would cause me to shake, cause me to fear him.

As he finished driving what felt like the millionth one in, the rope finally broke around my hands. My body flushed around, punching him in the face. I started to tear my feet, the ropes damaged from his boiling water stunt. Before I could get up, he kicked me hard in the face, a tooth flying off in the madness of the room.

I pulled him to the floor. His body landed in my chest, arms wrapped around my torso. "Remember when we first slept together, like this? My arms hugging you tight? You said you could only ever love me, that my ocean eyes held you in place." He stared back at me, his eyes seeming full with something. He was trying to catch me with his gaze as he'd done so many times before. When you have the perfect set of eyes, you can do just about anything.

Quickly, I pushed him off, getting up and limping away.

My leg hurt but I had to get out, had to leave these walls. I entered the kitchen first, a blue/green glow from the television lighting my path. I limped my way to our living room, the door only feet away. I rushed quickly as I saw it hit the door, a bottle of Jack Daniels flying faster than a baseball at a game. Glass spewed everywhere, cutting my face as I jumped back from the impact. The needles in my back making me uncomfortable, I grabbed the first thing I could find, an umbrella, and swung at him as he approached me.

"You will love me, goddammit," he screamed, the pointed tip of my weapon hitting his face. I jabbed it hard into his chest, knowing it wouldn't penetrate but at least be uncomfortable enough to get away. I grabbed the door handle and yanked it hard my way, but the door wouldn't open. The handle broke off as I tried to get out. I threw it at my attacker and limped out of the living room and toward our garage. He ran into the kitchen and grabbed a knife as I pushed through the door. I rushed to the car, trying to open the door, but they were locked.

He jangled the keys in front of me and slammed the door behind him. Setting the alarm, he caused red lights from the car to flush on in our darkness. As the car beeped twice I could see the yellow from the front end. I ran for the garage door, trying to lift it, but seeing it the handle bolted down. How long had he been planning this? I tried furiously again to open the car, to no avail. He slowly walked his way up to me, knife in hand. "You never gave us a chance! You gave up on us years ago, didn't you!" he screamed over and over.

Frustrated, I punched through the window of the passenger side and opened the door. Glass embedded in my navy fur. I couldn't see the blood oozing out from it, but I didn't have time to check it. I latched my fists to the car door to bring it my way. Riley got his hands caught in the path. Snow trapped in the cracks, he screamed again and shot back his arms, forcing the door to open slightly. I watched the keys fall from his hand to the floor and I thrust open the ajar door to grab them. Riley shot back up and tried to snatch them away. When I looked him in his eyes, I noticed the ocean was gone. There was no longer a blue sea waiting for its lover, only a wine dark beast thirsty to kill anyone who was brave enough to sail his waters.

Though he was white blur, I was faster. I slammed the door shut, jumped into the driver's seat. The moment I started that beast I put it in drive. My hand ached from the glass caught in my fur, but I didn't care. I needed to get out. He latched onto the broken window as I sped out of the house, tires blasting through the garage door. I saw Riley's body pulled away from the car by the impact as I made it outside. I stared for a moment, seeing his body twisted, unsure how damaged, if at all, he could be. The neighbors acres away, we were alone out there. As I was about to pull out of the driveway, I saw this white figure burst up. The bitch ran fast towards me, and all I could do was drive. His body flung onto the hood of my car; I reversed quick, causing him to hang tight. Under the moonlight, all I could see were the thin white arms attached to his body. Those eyes pierced through the windshield. I didn't want to find out what storms were happening inside.

When I stopped, he remained on. Riley was not about to let go. His skeletal claws clung tight to whatever they could find. So I put it in drive, speeding quick, tires screeching as we both moved forward. I made it to the edge of our street and stopped abruptly, the force finally causing him to let go. Before he could get up, I drove over him, hearing his bones crack underneath the weight of that beast. I ran back, then forward one last time, crushing whatever was left of his body as I sped off to somewhere. Anywhere. Just to get gone.

EATEN ALIVE

"So I suppose that's it, then?" She was furious. The blood of her fur stood on edge as I told her the news. Our TV created a thin veil of white noise between us as we stared awkwardly at each other. So many thoughts were rushing between us; memories, dinners, everything was so distant then. I ran my hand through the short fur on my head, breathing heavily to try and calm down; to try and weather the storm brewing in front of me. My chest extended, but it was minimal compared to what other animals could do. Meerkats were just small by nature; somedays I loathed it. "What should we do, Zack?" she asked finally. I could see the anger bubbling in her eyes. She stood there, expecting an answer. I could almost hear her thoughts as she glared at me. She had her arms crossed, her crimson fur meshing with the white of her chest. Her eyes squinted as she waited for the words to come through. Her claws were digging into her arms. The cat I once loved was seething with anger. For a moment, it felt as if she wanted to kill me, and that she had just the energy to do so.

"I don't know. I didn't mean for it to happen like this, Liz. I've been wanting to tell you for some time, now, but there's never been a good moment to do so. I haven't felt connected to you for almost a year. We barely talk anymore. Sex is an occasional affair." I let all the words come out at once. I let them attack her emotional fortress. I let them dig into her. I wanted her to know that this was more than jitters. The love was gone. "I need more in a relationship than just Netflix and a few gaming sessions. I need for us to be a couple. I'm afraid that's never going to happen again. I'm sorry."

"We're supposed to get married in two months. Zack, are we really going to cancel all this?" she asked me. I watched her look away. Glaring at the television.

"Yes," I responded.

"I don't feel so good. I'm going to take a shower," she followed, leaving the living room. I stared at the television, my mind a flurry of "what ifs." I let the news drown on in the background as I sat with myself, just thinking about what the future would look like. What being without her would look like. What just being would look like.

She had just started the shower as I decided to cook dinner. The news was still going, but I turned up the music as I started chopping vegetables and waited for the water to boil. I was plagued with the end of our relationship. The whole situation made me sick. I needed to leave, but at the same time I was still very attached to her. I knew I was making the best decision, but even the good ones pierce your gut like a blade. It was like the thought of us ending was a virus, crawling around in my blood. I was battling between myself. End it. Don't end it. But I had to endure. It was my decision. It was the right one. No matter how much it hurt, I had to endure. It was terrifying.

I changed the television and flipped on some music and let it pummel the air as I sliced through tomatoes briskly, though I was often never precise. I cut my finger with the knife while cutting and didn't notice until I was about to murder the onions. Crimson oozed all over my green fur before I started to run it through some cold water.

Steam was pouring out of the stove as the water finally boiled and like a shot through a guitar, I heard her scream. My tail stood firm as I ran towards the bathroom, her screams unstoppable by then. I burst through the door, nearly slipping from the impact.

My heart was moshing against my rib cage, my bones practically shaking as I scanned the room for anything out of the ordinary. Then I realized she was still behind the curtain.

"Babe, are you okay? I heard you screaming a moment ago," I said loudly, but got no answer. I could hear her breathing fast. Short, quick breaths about the speed of a double bass pedal. I didn't want to open the curtain, but I knew I had to. I knew I had to see what things lay behind it. I cursed myself for getting something dark. If it had been a brighter color, I might have been able to see what was happening with her shadow. I gripped the curtain, the water raining down. Its heat nearly burned my fur as I thrust it back open and saw it. Or them, really.

I saw her lying on the floor of the bathtub, her feline body ripped open by what seemed like little roaches, hundreds of them just devouring her white and red fur. The cross tattooed on her chest had split apart as those white devils mutilated her. When I looked in her eyes, they had already left us. Her body was alive, but she was dead. Liz was holding on by the weakness of her breath, but it wouldn't be long before she wholly left this world.

I said we were drifting apart. That I never felt connected to her. Seeing her like this made me feel strange; thoughts of our argument playing back in my head as these things roach-like insects ate away at her flesh stirred a sickening feeling inside me.

They were small, but God, were they strong in numbers.

Those long bodied bugs were chewing every inch of Liz away in front of me, chewing her down to bone. Their legs stretched out. Though they didn't have wings, one would think they did with how they jumped across from wall to wall. Some were coming out and going in our drains, others were escaping to the window. I had never seen them before, those strange insects. At first I wondered where they came from. The pipes? The air ducts? How did our home become infested with these unearthly creatures?

I had to sit and watch as her body was eaten alive. Tears started forming in my eyes as her breath got faster and faster. Her legs were being chewed off of her torso, one crawling away with a few underneath. Her belly burst open as more spilled out. Her blood was everywhere. Our beige walls were covered in every drop of it. I knew her end was coming. They were pouring out of her mouth now. Her whole head had been taken by then, eyes falling out of the sockets, ears gnawed away. They worked like ants, but those were far from ants. Ants wouldn't take a body like this. Ants wouldn't act this quickly.

Then I felt it. The illness that lingered in my body surged and I looked at my hand to see these little creatures crawling one by one from the cut on my finger. They were in me, my fur bubbling then like grass about to explode. My arms inflated, filled with whatever things were in me. It grew, my small frame enlarging. I felt them crawling all along my arm as my hand burst with them. From the mirror I could see all of my body just bulging in sections. I couldn't tell where the pain was coming from. Or even what the pain was. I just knew I was hurting real bad, as if I had broken all the bones in my body. Parts of my flesh were splitting open like a costume wrapped around a person too large to wear it.

I screamed in agony as I felt it. My cock had burst open. The bastards were funneling down my pants leg; my balls were soon to follow. My cheeks were bulging; my legs were being eaten. I would soon join her.

I flailed around in my bathroom. I didn't want to collapse yet. I didn't want to die. Not yet. I punched through the window and started to scream, but my throat wouldn't release my voice. They were working fast. They were eating me out from the inside.

How funny, to be eaten, ripped open and torn apart; I wondered if this was the new chapter of my life. Death. What lay beyond its veil was something I had yet to see, but I guessed I was coming for it then. I wondered what Liz saw when she passed over.

I stared at her body, bones exposed, her face half gone. Her fangs remained intact, as if they were the most resilient of her body. She always did know how to bite, but cats normally do when they're angry. I was lit up like Christmas, red and green bits all over me, our floor, everything. I couldn't stay up much longer. I was going down, and as I fell to the porcelain tile, I could hear others outside screaming. I could only assume because they were being devoured as well.

INTERLUDE 3

ABSOLUTION

Rachel followed Linus as he led her through what looked like an abandoned bar. Her stomach turned as she stared at the peeling wallpaper. Shivers ran through her body as fiber glass rubbed against her arm, and she worried if the floors would hold anybody in this home. Waving her hand through the smoky air, she started to speak. "Y'all ever thought of fixing the place up? Maybe getting a different color in here aside from purple?" she asked as she continued to follow closely to the tour guide.

Linus rolled his eyes at the complaints in her tone. "You sound so enthusiastic, darling." Linus was teasing. He knew she would eventually get tired of the journey; that he would have to change the course to keep her interested in the tour. Smoke and decay only went so far.

"Where is this smoke coming from anyways?" she responded, covering her mouth as she continued to push through the hallway. "Fuck!" she screamed as her body toppled over. She felt her feet tap something, and the moment her eyes looked back at them, she saw pool cues entangled between her ankles. "Man, leave it to me to get fucked up by trash."

Linus ignored all her complaints. He put out his hand to help her up, then started moving again when she got to her feet. "Well, to be honest, the hall is just about to take its turn for the worse," the goat said. A small giggle fell through his lips like spilled beer. He couldn't keep himself composed as they approached the lioness' path. A sense of dread started to brew inside of her. Although the giggle seemed innocent enough, she didn't feel the man with her was sane enough. Rachel had thought he was losing it, or maybe he had already lost his mind. Whatever the situation, she knew she wasn't comfortable.

A fit of laughter belted out of him. The hall filled to the brim with his maddening giggles. He hunched himself over and pointed forward, indicating where Rachel should go. Like a scared kitten, she walked cautiously. Her eyes fixated on the maniacal goat laughing his head away in the hall. "What the fuck is your problem?" she asked.

Linus didn't answer, simply laughing and pointing ahead. Not wanting to push it any further, Rachel jumped away from him and ran down the hall. Doors started to appear. She tried one, jiggling the handle only to find it locked. She frantically moved to another. Locked. On the third door, she pushed through. She took a moment to catch her breath, and let her eyes adjust to the room.

She couldn't believe her eyes when the door closed. Lit cigarettes and cigars filled the room with more smoke. She watched it trail under the crack of the doorway, realizing where it was coming from now. Beer glasses clanked and clamored around as the crowd inside the bar stumbled to the first seat available.

Rachel's eyes darted to the bartender, studying his face as

he pushed glasses to a group at the bar. There was a sad resolve in it, his pale blue fur dwindling in color every second she stared at him. Whatever hope he carried was nearly gone, as if the rabbit's fate was held here and he wasn't going to leave. She started to look at other faces. A fox smoking at a booth held his face down in an empty glass, a candle flickering next to him as his fingers ran around the ring. A lioness danced in the corner, her face swollen with tears as her hips moved slow with the rhythm of the music. Rachel felt everything the room was carrying all at once, and she knew there was nothing but sadness there. Each animal she looked at, each person's face she made eye contact with, she could feel the weight of their sadness pressing down on her shoulders. She could see the color fading every time she looked around. Immediately, she knew all life had left that bar before it could even enter. "They are all damned," she said under her breath.

"Come to drink with the dead?" a man asked her. It took a moment for the lioness to see him, but when her vision finally fixated on the short turtle before her, she nodded.

"You're all dead here?" she asked in return. She studied the shell of the turtle first, then fixated on how shriveled his arms looked. *The green was almost gone from him, too,* she thought. *I guess that's what happens when you die. You lose the color you carried with you.*

He waved his hand, motioning her to follow him. Rachel's eyes looked around at the crowd that surrounded her, each drinking something she couldn't decipher.

"That doesn't look like alcohol," she said as the pair made it to the back of the bar. She then saw a chip on the turtle's shell, exposing flesh underneath. Trying not to show she noticed it, she took a seat at the table. Her guide pulled a martini glass and held it to his eyes. A thick liquid started to ooze from the corners of his eyes. Muffled groans and whines escaped his mouth as he let the green oozing liquid fill the glass to the rim.

"Everything about us is a reminder of our past. We are damned, as you muttered under your breath moments ago. So everything we do is so that we never forget the sins we've committed. This is our fate. We are here, trying to find a way to move on, so we must drink of our life. Each sorrow is supposed to show us the way to rest, but it is not an easy task." The turtle moved his head slowly to the full bar.

A glass shattered and Rachel watched as a tiger flipped a table. No one tried to stop him as he destroyed the chairs and floors around him. "Fuck!" Rachel shook as he screamed. She watched as this nude feline reduce everything in front of him to pieces. Splinters embedded themselves into his body as his fist continued to pummel into the wood pile he created. "I can't do it! I can't fucking take it anymore! I just want to live, Goddamnit!" He screamed some more, tears leaving his eyes like a river. They all followed the same stream, connecting as they hit the ground and inching their way to his glass.

"Some of us can't keep it together, unfortunately." She heard the age in his voice. The pair continued to watch the tiger demolish the wood for a few moments longer until the bartender approached. The rabbit placed his pale blue hand on the tiger's shoulder, then grabbed the full glass of the feline's tears and put it in his hand. "That tiger is a destructive creature, even in death. Behind the doors of his home, he would beat his partners, what few he had, anyways. So Linus stripped him bare, as he stripped his partners of everything when he was with them. He'll stay here for a long time."

The bartender approached the pair and left a glass and a drink mixer on the table. Taken aback, she stared at his crotch, seeing he was without pants. She studied the cage that was locked on the bunny's groin, seeing the rods that were piercing his penis. "Ronald has been here the longest. He put the cage on himself. A Mormon when he was alive, he preached so hard against same sex couples. He's been here the longest, so he serves us while he drinks from his own secretive life. He just wants to stop being aroused, but unless he lets go of his "holy" preachings, he'll be here forever. You are not dead, therefore you must drink the life of someone who is dead." The turtle poured the first cocktail and pushed it her way.

Rachel reluctantly grabbed the glass, looking around to see everyone else drinking, sobbing—remembering. She brought the glass to her lips and took one big gulp. Her vision blurred. "Don't worry, it'll be a quick sensation. Happens to us all at first." The turtle's voice was fading farther away from her. Before she could respond, everything went black.

MADNESS VASE

I don't know when the madness set it, or if it was even madness that took him away. I know whatever thing took hold of my lover, its twisted nature oozed out of his fur. Life comes at you so fast, some days all you see are blurs. Until you need to reach out for a specific memory, the moments you live are all just splotches of time held; sometimes you hold onto them for too long, keeping the smudge painted over that moment in your brain, unable to filter through and see the clear picture. But when I look back at him, I see him as clear as a reflection in the water. Perfect. With ripples.

The sky-tinted fur meshed with the cloudy splotches on his belly and muzzle. When he brushed his hands over the grape haze of my arms, I thought clouds were reaching out to me. But the sky didn't stay blue for long.

He hated when I made fun of the way he talked. Noah could never control his tongue. Sometimes, it would just slip out, adding extra syllables to words that never needed them. It was like he was adding his own spin to a misunderstood language.

I hated the way he drank beer from the side of the can

like a frat boy. He said he liked it better that way, I always thought he just liked chewing on the can as the bitter liquid invaded his mouth. I guessed some habits were hard to crack. I never understood the fascination with cans, but Noah never understood my fascination with socks. What's a ferret to do though? I mean, they're soft as fuck! Who doesn't like socks? It's like saying you don't like The Beatles (which Noah continued to tell me. Prick).

We just moved in together. A hard move for me, as I lived hours away from him. We had to drive halfway just to see each other some weekends. I know when you're only dating for about a year, it can be a dodgy choice, but there was just something about that goat that got to me. There was always a softness in his eyes. They were so yellow, as if they were miniature suns, just staring back at you.

So I packed my sock collection and threw it right into his apartment. If that odd homely goat loved me, he was just going to have to handle my strange addictions as I handled his.

But things started to get weird. I don't know how to quite explain it, but it's like he left me to care for his body, his mind venturing off. The morning it started was normal.

I had just gotten out of the shower and stared at myself in the mirror. The dark purple of my hand soothed the lighter shade of my belly. "Yo, what's taking so long?" he yelled as he bolted through the door, horns first. Goats had a weird sense of pushing things. He rammed his head on anything that was in his way when he wanted to. I stood there nude, drying off, bits of purple shedding from my body as I ran the towel over me. He wore a coy look on his face, bringing his hand to my hips, then to my belly. "You're not thinking of losing a pound or two, are you?" *Bitch*, I remember thinking. He worked real hard to keep me from the gym. Said he liked his men plump.

I scoffed and pushed him playfully off me. "Are you sure

this is even going to be worth it?" I asked and he grabbed the print out he found on Facebook. He had this terrible habit of keeping all the useless adverts he got on there as he "wanted to keep them in case we got bored." I mean, what the fuck is the internet for? Am I wrong?

"It's going to be epic! Listen, I saw this online and people have started posting on all the weird stuff they found! One guy posted on Reddit that he found this old doll. He was afraid of it being haunted. Just think of what we could find!" I threw on some clothes and then rolled my head in a sigh.

"Whatever it was you just said, was the gayest thing to pop out of your mouth. Legit." It was difficult for me to see the excitement he held. His fur prickled as his mind turned over the sensation of hunting for weird shit. What really got to me was that it was in a graveyard! *Like, seriously, the shit there is haunted; you're grave robbing!* But I pushed it all aside. I hadn't seen his eyes get so lively before. It was like the day I asked if we could move in—a look I hoped he'd look like when I asked him to marry me. There was so much fire in his eyes. I remember thinking how the sky had never looked so blue before. It was a Texas sky, all blue, all sun—all alive.

He threw on his jacket and set his glasses on his face. Kissing me on my cheek, he whispered in my ear, "I'll buy you lunch." Bitch knew just how to get to me. That motherfucker knew if he said food, I'd trot along behind him because a ferret's gotta eat. I was not about to go hungry.

I groaned and rolled my eyes. "Fine, but I'm picking the place this time," I said, smacking his ass. We both ran out chuckling to the car. As I plopped in the passenger, I looked up at the building. I could see our window from the ground. There was a strange figure standing, but I couldn't put it together. It was just a blur. A splotch. I closed my eyes and when I opened them again, it was gone.

The place was dead. And I mean that in every way possible. The sun was sitting right in the middle of the sky, but that wasn't a sign to the rest of nature to say, "Hey, maybe it shouldn't be cold today." But whatever.

We pushed past the gates. I stared at them as they towered over me; gothic pieces of steel standing upright from the ground, remaining open, yet so unwelcoming. He parked the car at the front, his eyes staring at me from the side. He had this slight smirk on his face, the kind of smirk that begged to fuck. Though it felt like we were alone, I felt a hint of someone's presence watching us. A glance around as I stepped out of the car showed no one. Zipping up my jacket, I pushed myself closer to him and kissed his cheek. "Lunch better be damn good, fuckboy."

Noah held my arm close to him. I could feel his body shake as he chuckled. "Oh, we're on that level now. I thought we was closer than that." The words left his mouth playfully. My hand snatched his tongue as it stayed on the side of his lips. We tread over the first hill. My eyes scanned through the graves, noticing the legacy of families buried closely together. Generations covered the top end of the hill. My legs felt as if they were stumbling over misplaced rocks and mud. Not my idea of adventure, but sometimes I couldn't say no to his face.

We walked up to a small wooded area. It was enough to not be seen, while being completely visible. It's weird how trees and grass cover someone who is barely hiding. He knelt down behind a bush, digging rapidly. His hand dove right into the bush, not caring if it got sliced by thorns. His face wore the strain as the bush rattled. Then, when everything stopped, his eyes got soft again. He yanked his hand out fast, holding up the newly obtained item as if he were a character from a video game. A steel flask showed in the sun, the dim item clutched tight in Noah's hand. "Told you, Alex! This is fucking epic!" The excitement from his voice was shattering for a moment. I had never seen him get this happy before, not since I'd moved in.

I gave him a faint smile, brushing my hand over his arm. He handed me the flask and nodded for me to open it. I remember how hard it was to just pull it open, the cork nearly cemented in the top. I'd always hated how corks felt in my hands. The pieces that broke off made my fur feel as if bugs were lingering on my body. When I finally yanked it out, I tossed the cork away, frustrated with how difficult it had been to deal with. I quickly turned the flask over, shaking out whatever contents into my dark purple palm. I remember a small bit of paper inching out, rolled fat like a blunt. And yes, if your friend is giving you skinny ass joints, they're a shitty friend. Make some new ones—ones who don't bogart the weed. Just saying.

My stubby fingers rolled open the fat wad from the flask. Noah snatched the silver container from me as I read the words: "Will you marry me?" I wasn't ever really sure how I imagined being proposed to, or if I ever imagined it at all. The wind pushed gently through the trees; I remember the faint rustling behind us as I tried to push my heart down my throat. My eyes darted over those words, as if the ink would disappear if I blinked.

My body spun around so quick, I practically tackled him to the ground. "Fuck yes," I exclaimed, latched to his body as if he would float away. As if everything that just happened would reset and the message would be nothing more than a simple "Love you." I felt him stumble beneath me as I stretched my neck to kiss him, and in that moment we tumbled to the cold, soft grass, fortunate enough not to hit the grave stone we were invading.

He said nothing as he grabbed my ass. His hand slid beneath my hands, grabbing my bare cheek. I could feel his cock beneath me. Opening my eyes, I tried to assess the risk, but he didn't even bother, pulling my shirt over my head and tossing it aside. My pants weren't on for too long either as he stripped me. I stood up, he pushed me over the headstone of that grave and thrusted his cock inside me.

I could hear his tongue lull out of his mouth as his hips thrust hard against me. He was a lot of things, but underwhelming was never one of them. I didn't believe there were perfect sizes for cocks, but if there was one his would have been it. The fur of his paws meshed with my hips as he grew faster. I couldn't keep myself from moaning, each time his dick thrust against my prostate. Though my eyes were drunk, I still tried to let them wander, tried to see if we'd get caught here in the open, but the goat would turn my attention back to him. His hands grabbing my bulge, pulling my head back, smacking my ass. He held me hostage there in that moment of exhibitionism. I moaned the words, "I love you" syncopated with each thrust. My hands gripped that gravestone hard, the gravel moving around the flesh beneath my purple haze.

I knew he was getting close. I was getting closer. My orgasm erupted quick underneath his grasp, my seed shooting hard against whoever's headstone that was. Apologizing mentally, I could feel his hips get faster, harder, his grip tighter now. I knew it was coming. And as the wind blew against our bodies, I felt the warmth of his cum filling me.

The wind picked up as we gathered ourselves together. The weather there rarely stayed good for long. I could never tell what it was, but every other day it seemed a storm started to settle in. Clouds inched their way over us as we started to leave. I was surprised at how unseen we really had been, but then how many people came to visit a graveyard? Still, when the excitement was over, when the rush left our bodies, I couldn't help but feel uneasy. As if the universe had seen us and planned some inevitable punishment. Or maybe an actual ghost.

I'd never really been superstitious, but when I looked back, I thought I saw the audience that was there with us that day.

Snow was moving in fast. Winter was a harsh master when he settled in town, and although I'd have given anything to see the warm summers of the south, I knew the snow would bind me there. But weather is rarely important when you're in love.

There was a feeling inside our home, an uneasy tension that kept us both on edge, kept us both at the ledge of strangling each other. I know we were both stressed. He was carrying the bills while I looked for work, and managing my job hunt seemed like a battle lost before it started. I knew the mess going in. Starting a new life isn't just an easy drive. But when he came home some nights, there was a look in his eyes when he glanced at me. A look that twisted my stomach into a mass of rubber bands.

It was raining when we had our millionth fight on the issue. He came in soaked and I had just started making dinner. He dropped his coat on the floor, water splattering like blood patterns against the walls.

"How was work, love?" I stirred the soup nervously, the broth boiling now. The steam poured over my face as he set his keys on the counter.

"It was fine. How was your day?" The words weren't exactly cold. There was a touch of warmth on his tongue as he loosened his tie from his neck. It was odd, but I stopped stirring and looked at him.

"It was fine. I had an interview today." His eyes rolled as the words fell off my tongue like droplets of grease.

"And I bet you botched that one too."

"That's not entirely fair, babe. I felt it went alright this time. I at least knew what I was talking about. They said they'd call me back." I placed my hand on his and tried to stroke upward, but he pulled away. It was like a quick strike of blue lightning. Bit of fur jumped from his hand and danced playfully in the unsettling air. It was a brief jolt screaming not to touch him. I wanted to stroke his horns, bring him back to me as this was not the Noah I'd grown to love. That body in front of me was just a shell, going through changes, getting rid of everything that made him Noah and replacing him with...with a monster.

There was a sternness in his eyes. A strong presence I hadn't seen before. It was like you stared into them and saw the dark wintry anger wafting around his body. It chilled me. I took a step back, leaned against the kitchen counter, still facing him, and said, "Hey, what's wrong?"

He shook his head, as if he had just been in a daze. It was like his mind was dreaming of a war not fought, the guns blaring in his ears as he stood there. I wondered for a moment if he even heard me, or if he knew I was there. "I'm just tired, babe. I'm gonna go strip off these clothes and sleep for a bit." His body stumbled slowly to the bedroom. I knew he wasn't drunk. His breath hadn't emitted the scent. His mind was genuinely gone. Like it left to go to the store, and forced the body to fend for itself.

I watched him wander down the hall, the bedroom light flushed on, but it didn't stay on for long.

I ate my soup—-the whole time restless. I felt as if I was being watched, but I didn't look behind. If I was, I knew it'd be him, and I didn't want to dive into another argument or discussion, or whatever. I would let him watch. I would eat. Browse for jobs. But I would not give him the gift of my fear.

I didn't sleep in the same bed with him that night.

I slept on the couch that night. I had one small cover, barely enough to cover my body, but the room was hot. Or cold. Or whatever my body felt during sleep. It was uncomfortable regardless. It had to have been about two, maybe three in the morning when I felt it. My back was turned to the air, face against the back of the couch. I had a leg on the floor because I slept weird and it was the couch. But nevertheless I remember my body feeling numb. I tried to move my hand or arms, but I couldn't. It was like I was completely paralyzed. Stuck on that couch when I really had to pee.

Then I heard it. A large thud that made the purple in my fur leave me, creating a pale frozen ferret. It was like a hammer being driven through drywall. It knocked once, but my brain couldn't help to imagine the sheetrock break apart, dust spiraling off as a piece was severed from the foundation.

It pounded again, the apartment giving a small echo beneath the sounds of the wind.

Again. This time closer. I wanted to look behind me. I wanted to see whatever the fuck it was that was causing me to stay frigid on that damnable couch, but I couldn't move a limb.

It pounded one more time, right behind me, as if inches away. I could hear it breathing, a low rumbling breath as if it had nothing but fluid in its lungs. I started to feel its breath right on my neck and moving up. The hot air ticked me as it made it up my ear.

My breathing increased; I could feel my chest pounding against my rib cage each time I exhaled. It placed a hand on my shoulder and gripped it firmly, the darkness covering the identity of my guest. It pulled me close to its ear and whispered, "Sleep." And like that, it was gone.

When I awoke the next morning, the feeling was gone. As if whatever aura that entangled our home had just vanished. Noah was just waking up; I could hear him stretching in our bedroom. The goat was monstrous when pushing out of sleep. Most mornings he would push his arms out as if reaching for the sky while drowning, a large growl emitting from his out. The walls nearly rumbled each time it happened. I learned to sleep through it over time.

I pushed off the couch and started making coffee. Placing the pot in the sink, I ran the water through it before filling it whole. I left the water running as I started the maker, grabbing a sponge and scrubbing dishes. After the night before, I didn't want to look at him much. I was still shaken from the whole night, and I had believed he was the thing that was messing with me on the couch.

His footsteps made a loud thud on the carpet. Though muffled, you could still hear the floor wanting to give out beneath the blue beast. He was odd. Noah was never a too heavy of a person, but he could never step lightly onto anything. Every step he made was just another crash after crash. It was like he wanted to destroy tiny cities that lived there like in a giant monster movie. He made his way into the kitchen and grabbed a mug.

"Good morning, babe," he said, kissing me on the cheek.

"Good morning; how'd you sleep?" I responded, still scrubbing what little dishes we had in the sink.

"Ugh, terrible! I thought you were fucking with me last night while slept. I kept hearing something in the room whispering, but nothing coherent. It was fast, ranty almost. I felt it over on your side of the bed, so I figured it was just you. I got up, took a piss and moseyed into the living room, only to find you asleep on the couch. It was honestly kind of freaky. I moved in close to you and felt your shoulder and you were tense. I through you were having a bad dream, but didn't want to wake you. So I went back to bed and, well, the whispering started up again. I flipped on the light and still nothing. I couldn't figure it out but fuck it was freaky and annoying." His story made my fur stand up. It was more than likely him who said "sleep" in my ear, but it was more than just a touch I felt.

"Maybe we have a ghost?" I said teasingly. I wanted to lighten the air between us. I knew he had been stressed to no end, so a quick laugh of any kind would do him some good.

"What do you think it wants?" he asked flatly. It was the kind of tone that didn't tell you anything. He could have still been angered from last night, or he could be totally fine now. I turned off the water from the sink and started to pour a cup of coffee.

"Maybe it's a pirate, and he's after some primo-goat booty!" I said, taking a brief sip and scanning his face. Still. Cold. Nothing.

"Ghosts are legit; you know that, right?" he asked as he held out his mug, expecting me to pour his coffee for him.

I simply nodded to the maker and enjoyed my cup. "I've always been on the fence about them, honestly. I don't want to say they're fake because, let's be real, it would be so awesome if we found a ghost." Noah just shook his head. It was like the sky twirling back and forth, his horns whisking the air.

"I don't think you should be joking about something so serious, Alex. I'm starting to think you were doing last night on purpose." You could feel the annoyance in his voice, like a power surge that spread across your body through his voice.

"You think I did this? After you practically manhandled me last night?" I was pissed. I knew the words shouldn't have left, but I let them go. "I heard your breathing against me. I felt your hand. I heard you say 'sleep,' Noah. I wasn't messing with you last night, but I'm damn well convinced you were fucking with me." He looked at me, stunned as if I would even say anything like that about him.

"I don't think you understand everything I'm doing for you. I go out there, every day..."

"And you fucking work! But that still doesn't give you the right to do what you did last night." My voice was growing. Each letter was a new tree sprouting in a forest along my tongue. My anger—the soil of this growing world inside me.

"I didn't fucking do it!" The words were a roar now. I could see he wanted to throw his mug at me with every bit of strength in his body. But he restrained himself.

"Then who did?" There wasn't a word from his mouth afterward, and I was not easing up.

There was a hell inside of him. A hell I hadn't seen before. A hell that lay dormant until the surrounding world came to badger it awake. And this was that time. You can love someone to death, but sometimes the hell they carry inside them is too much to bear. When his fires started to burn my flesh, I knew our clock was counting down. I just didn't know how much time we had left before we'd split apart.

Weekends were never an easy venture. We were stuck in the same home; the same walls, the same kitchen, maybe a room apart, but when you're only a door away, you feel every bit of their presence. But it wasn't just us. I kept getting this feeling that there was something else with us. Something that we just couldn't see. I wanted to believe that he was not the monster he was becoming, or the anger that was carried in his coffee mugs. He still has a perfect image in my mind. His scars are only cosmetic. My bruises are only meant to heal. Pain is only temporary. Even when all life is suffering, pain is only temporary.

He was working at his computer in our bedroom. We hadn't talked since that morning. I had never seen him grip his mug so tight before; I knew he was on the verge of breaking down. I don't know if he ever stopped balancing that ledge. Or if I ever saw the edge he was teetering on. You paint your lover in fulfillment, in love, ignoring the flaws and the sense of danger that follows them. Whenever I looked at my little goat boy, I only saw the bluest sky. As if the real deal that hovered over us both couldn't measure up. He was the sky I wanted in my life. As painful as it sounds.

He emerged from the bedroom around lunch time. Annoyance hung in his eyes like lingering tears. We exchanged a glance, then I went back to my book. I didn't want to say anything to him. I didn't want to know he existed in this room. I just wanted quiet.

"Is there anything to eat?" the words fell flat from his lips.

I didn't look up from my book. I could see his figure from the corner of my eye, blurred blue standing tall in kitchen. "I'm sure there's something in the fridge, babe. Just have to look."

"Oh, fuck you! If you didn't want to answer, you should have just stayed quiet." I heard the door forced open. For a moment, I thought I could see something else in the kitchen with him. A blurred figure, just grey. I knew the blue was moving around, but the grey just stood there. The door slammed shut as he started making something. I didn't bother looking. I was focused on this visible, yet invisible mark wedged between us both.

"I'm sorry, babe." My words were silent, yet loud enough for him to hear. That's what fear does to you. It mutes your voice.

"You're always fucking sorry." I heard him say as he slammed his plate against the counter. How it didn't break was a miracle.

"Well, I wouldn't be if I weren't made to feel like an inconvenience all the time!" I threw the book onto the floor and stood up before him.

"Oh, so I make you feel like an inconvenience, is that it? Let's not forget what I do for us." His eyes stared intently at my heart. It was as if he knew he carried daggers in them, that he could use them to pierce what frail flesh I wore. "Maybe if you found some fucking work, I wouldn't have to be so fucking stressed all the time." His voice grew louder. The walls bounced his words between them. "You know what? Maybe...if you can't fucking appreciate the hell I..."

Cutting him off, a coffee mug was thrown at him like a baseball pitch winning the world series. The cup shattered as it hit the cabinet, bits of glass spewing outward and back at him. I couldn't tell if he was injured, shunning my eyes away, flinching upon impact.

There was a third person among us. A third, invisible presence causing this tension. Yet even though we were not alone, not causing the turmoil we were suffering through at that moment, he still thought these things of me. There wasn't a ghost more frightening than that.

It didn't get easier the next day. Noah sent me out to get a few groceries while he stayed behind and "thought through" what had happened. He wouldn't talk about the cup; wouldn't mention how it flew or where it went after it landed. He just needed space to think. He kept saying I needed to get gone for him to have peace for a few hours.

Noah had been growing worse by the hour. Or at least it felt that way. Every time he moved around me, my fur stood on edge. It used to soften by his touch, but the more anger that seeped from his body, the more I wanted to get away.

I was convinced that this presence in our home was bringing out the worst in him. All those evils carried in his heart, bleeding out by this invisible pest. That wasn't the same goat I fell in love with. It wasn't the same goat that proposed to me. It was like his body was being taken over, like our infestation was carving him out inside in order to make itself home. But what was home to something paranormal?

Our lights were off when I got home. I set the groceries on the counter, the kitchen not far from the front door. I could hear a faint whimpering in the bedroom. The sun peered through the window, lighting what pieces of our living room it could reach. I slowly removed my scarf and out of my nervousness wrapped it around my hand. I wanted to say something. Anything. Just a syllable to stop the whimpering, but I said nothing as I approached the bedroom.

I clutched my scarf tight as I poked my head through the doorway. And then I saw him. Naked. My blue goat boy on his knees as this figure held his shoulders. It was whispering in his ear. I couldn't hear it, but I knew it was whispering. There was an evil in that room that I could not bear to remain in front of, but I could see Noah's life draining within moments.

Noah, I don't know what you expected of me. But I jumped in, grabbed his shoulders and yanked him from the beast. Only he didn't come with me. His head rammed into my belly, horns almost piercing me as I was thrust into the wall. I couldn't get back up. I didn't even know if I wanted to get back up. It was the first time he had hurt me like that. My eyes widened at the blue fur that hovered over me. I thought he'd kick me, but he only went back to the bedroom.

As this beast took everything about him away from me, I lost what energy I had. Everything went black.

When I awoke, he was in our bed, lying there as I saw him then. The color of the sky didn't last forever. Some days it was more gray than blue, and when it was truly blue there was still a sliver of decay hidden inside it. I sat there for what seemed like days, but it was only hours, thinking he'd move, but he never responded to my touch. He lay before me, only a shell. A breathing body left in a coma by what has entered our home.

Rain tapped the roof of our home. Thunder was low, but

audible. The silent rains were always the worst. They were always the ones that hit hard as they moved inward. I didn't know what the sky had in store for us, but I knew it wasn't going to be an easy rain.

I wondered if that thing had come from our adventure in the graveyard, or if that spirit was the lingering hatred between us. But what good were answers then when the dead had woven your path? Like lavender traveling through a polluted ocean, I rubbed my hand across his thigh, eased it along his torso. The rest of my body followed, engulfed in the murky blue that was him. When I reached the headrest, I pulled him into me. There was a longing to gain back what I had lost, yet a fear of what I would actually receive if he opened his eyes. And that's when I saw it.

This shadowy beast sat in the corner of our room, watching us intently. Lightning illuminated it every other minute. There was a craze in his eyes, as if it had been waiting for that. We were its prey and it had been hunting us for what seemed like forever. I wanted to move, but I couldn't get my body to push away from my lover lying dormant. It was as if our bed was an ocean and the shore was too far to swim to. I was paralyzed in that room, stuck there to suffer whatever fate that beast had planned for us. Noah's arms started to wrap around me as if twine could wrap without help. A small groan left his throat as he squeezed me against his body. I was caught. Noah's grip kept me in place, his arms crushing my upper body. I had never seen sky envelop a purple haze in my life, but he was doing his best to swallow me whole.

"Stop." My voice finally let the words go. My lips pushed the letters out and before I could say anything else, his body was on top of me, his hands strangling my throat. Noah's eyes shot open, a swollen numbness hanging on his face as his grip got tighter. I thrust my hands up, grabbing his horns, then his face, struggling to break free from my lover's grip. I didn't want to hurt him. I didn't want him to suffer anything, though he was strangling me. It wasn't him; it wasn't really him. He was the puppet for that beast in our room.

That wasn't the Noah that I loved, the goat boy on his knees with the ring. When I saw him, really saw him, he was an ocean of love. I swam through his waves each night I was with him. That boy made my fur glow, a lavender neon light that could not come alive without his touch, as if he held the switch to my bulb.

I didn't recognize the body above me. I didn't know who had been living with me all those months. I could feel the air leave my body. My arms started to grow weak as I pushed them away from him. I felt along our nightstand, fingers weakly grabbing onto the first thing they could. A set of keys jingled violently as I thrust them up into his eye.

He wailed loudly, his hands leaving my throat. A rush of air punched me in the gut as I tried to roll off the bed. Lightning flashed outside, the walls lit up as it struck close to our home.

When I stood up I saw the beast behind him, his arms outstretched with Noah's. My future husband now a doll, they had me cornered. I grabbed our lamp from the nightstand and threw it hard at the pair. They dodged quickly and I ran for the door.

My legs bolted through and ran into our kitchen. Shaking, I ripped open drawers and started searching for anything to stop the two from killing me. Silverware littered our floor; a parade of clanking metal on cold tile erupted throughout our home.

When he entered our kitchen, I threw a plate. Glass spewing from the impact, I started throwing everything, anything to keep him away. Like a soldier, he made his way towards me in the narrow walkway. Trapped again, I grabbed a knife and shoved it into his belly. I pushed past him again and ran into the bathroom, locking the door.

I ripped open the mirror door and looked for the lighter we kept. He hated matches, wanting candles. That was the one time I was thankful we didn't have a normal air freshener in our home. I grabbed the small device and a can of hairspray.

Loud bangs erupted at the door. He pounded furiously, trying hard to burst through. Slowly, I could see the door break from its hinges. The wood splintered with each forceful punch. I could imagine he was thinking of punching me, or maybe the demon was thinking of it. I couldn't tell anymore. There was one thing I knew about that night. The beast was real. My love was not as cruel, never as cruel as he was. But that was never him. It was this thing. Twisting us. Controlling us, marionette puppets entertaining it when it wanted us too.

I was trapped there. There was only one thing left for me then. Blue skies still have to see another day. So I aimed the lighter and hairspray as the door flew into the wall. He screamed loudly, this blue angered body running in like a zombie. Before he could see me, I started the lighter. It took a few tries. Gas station lighters were the worst, but they were cheap. The moment the flame lit he turned around, eyes narrowing at me. "Let him go," I told whatever was inside him. There was a storm overhead; I heard the winds howling between us as I stood armed. "I don't know what you want, or why you're here. I don't care." The storm raged behind us then. The air was still, as if time had frozen it. "You can have me instead. Let Noah go, and I'll give myself to you."

I could see the creature pondering the proposal behind my fiancé. Its eyes narrowed as if thinking, but it wasn't long before Noah's body lifted in the air. I could see blue skies falling away from me as the creature flung towards my body. I struggled for a moment as it felt like it was trying to take control of my body.

Noah was slowly coming to, his body trying to lift itself

from the floor. I tried fighting it; tried keeping it from taking hold of my arms. I wasn't going to be its puppet. The lighter had blown out, but I struck it again, this time lighting it with two hits. I turned the can to me and yelled to Noah, "Babe! You need to get out! Don't look here; just go." Noah was still trying to regain consciousness. I could see him sitting up, but he wasn't aware of anything yet.

"What's going on?" I heard him ask.

I didn't have time to waste. I screamed out to him, as the beast held onto me with more force than I could really handle. "I love you!" And I sprayed the can towards my face, my body lighting on fire. Flames engulfed my arms, my chest, my face, everything. My fur was burning, but I could hear its screams. It was in pain; like I was in pain. Like I'd been in pain since it arrived.

As the fire took us both, I became the dawn. A purple morning preparing all for the storm that was heading for them. I was slowly losing consciousness, but I saw him in a blur. He was running for me, but, babe, it was too late. We were gone. We are gone. I love you.

HOW WELL YOU WALK
THROUGH DEATH

He sat on the driver's side of my car. I could feel the wind rustle through my fur as it picked up. I was walking up to the vehicle as he neared the edge of that cliff. The skies wore their pale grey well. Everything felt slow. My steps felt as if I were walking through mud, but I could see the blinding green grass beneath me. I could see his head, the long dark void that sprouted at the top and lingered down to his shoulders, a pale auburn muzzle sticking outward as he stared at the sea in front of us.

"What are you doing with my car?" I shouted at him, looking through the back window. I thought I could see something on the inside, but it was only my reflection. I watched for a moment, hoping to see his eyes, his mouth, anything to confirm it was Logan. I hadn't seen him or heard from him in months. Not since we'd broken it off last summer.

I looked around us, wondering how we even got there. Where was that? The golden yellow of my fur shone bright beneath those pale grief-stricken skies. I ran my hand through my mane, bits of darkened brown latching to my fingers.

I finally walked my way to the driver's side, where he was, and tried to open the door. It was locked. I pounded a fist against the window, but it didn't shake him. I tried screaming, but the air made it feel muffled. I pounded and screamed again and again until he finally looked my way.

And when I saw his face, every bit of my core plummeted to the deepest part of my belly. His eyes were gone, blood streaming down his face. He took a finger, dipped it in the crimson and started writing something on the window. I couldn't move. I wanted to look away, but I was too entranced by what he was writing. I had to know, I had to see what he was trying to tell me.

But all he wrote was, "Your fault."

The car moved forward, and I watched it inch over the cliff. What exactly was my fault? "Wait!" I shouted after him, grabbing onto the bumper. He didn't stop; he drove us both down over the cliff. My hulky body fell along with him, but before I could even reach the ground, I shot up from my bed.

My breath was heavy. I felt my chest swelling to take in every bit of air that surrounded me, only to force it out in one large huff over and over. It had only been a dream, but goddamn, had it felt some kind of real. I looked around the room as my eyes adjusted to the darkness. A warm hand grabbed my belly, smoothing along my fur downward.

"Did you have a nightmare, babe?" the voice of my partner oozed out, a sleep-filled garble latched to each of their words. I grabbed their hand and kissed it, lying back as I started to calm down.

"I don't know what it was, love. It was somethin'" I said as I rolled to face them. Before I could kiss their forehead, I saw they were fast asleep again. Their soft pink fur stood out amidst the darkness, almost giving a neon glow to their body. Vic was never one to stay awake for long after sleep had taken them. Their green hair lay sporadically over their face. Vic never wore it long, but the raccoon always said they liked to have some style. I never quite understood, but my hair was wild by nature. Lion manes were meant to grow thick; I wouldn't trim mine for the world. Smiling faintly, I planted a kiss on their silver mask and tried to go back to sleep, though I only kept replaying the dream. How green the grass was, how surreal the blood and the lack of eyes. It shook me. My spine wavered at the sight that kept popping back into my mind. I wanted to know what it meant. What did he mean when he said it was my fault?

I had half a mind to call him, but I knew it wouldn't solve anything. Why call someone for something that happened in a dream?

After a few minutes I realized I wasn't going back to sleep. The world held me hostage and lying in bed started to itch in my skull. I needed to do something, otherwise I'd be restless the rest of the day.

I inched my way out while Vic slept, their breath letting out tiny snores. I walked into our kitchen and started a pot of coffee, grabbing my phone off its charger. I started to thumb through my Twitter notifications and my timeline only to stop when I saw his picture on my screen. The auburn fox with black hair stared right at me with a short message. It just read "Goodbye." Logan was always dramatic. Everything he did had that added annoying flair to it. He would leave twitter a million times only to return the next day. Although taking in my dream, I wondered if the message meant something else.

I tried to push him out of my mind as I poured my coffee. Before I could set my phone down, it started to vibrate. The time said 04:30 a.m. Although I wondered who the fuck would call me this early, I had a feeling I knew who and why I was getting this call. I was quick to answer, setting my coffee down. "Hello?" I said, my voice still carrying an air of exhaustion from just waking up.

"Axel?" Her voice sounded rough on the phone. As if she had been crying for days. I knew what she was about to say.

"Melanie?" I asked, though I knew it was her.

"He's dead, Axe." She was choking up on the phone. I could hear the tears forming in her eyes and wondered if she'd be able to say anything else.

"When?"

"We found him a couple hours ago. He hung himself. A mother should never have to find her son hanging like he was." A long wail escaped the speaker through my phone. I couldn't say anything. My body frozen in the kitchen, I wanted to try and console her, but what was there to say then? My brain scrambled for words. It felt like picking nails from a pile of screws. Finally, my brain mustered up some form of courage to respond to her constant crying.

"I'm sorry, Melanie." The words stumbled out of my lips.

"I'll—text—you—the details—" she said between large huffs of air. Grief had taken her fully, wrapped its arms around her body and it was not about to let go. Before I could respond, she hung up the phone, leaving me to my coffee and the silence of my home.

"I don't want you to go alone." Vic said as I told them the news. I was working on my third cup of coffee; I took a long sip thinking about what they were saying, what the words were implying.

"I don't know if you should go. I'm not even sure if I want to go." I let the words trail off as I took a seat on our couch.

"I mean, you were married to him for almost a decade, love. It's okay to go. He may have been a bastard, but he was a part of your life." They sat down next to me and started to rub my shoulders. "I'm just saying I'm going with you."

I couldn't look at Vic. My mind was too far away from

the raccoon. I felt as if I were adrift, just me and the universe all analyzing the dream I'd had. I didn't want to believe Logan wanted to kill himself. I didn't even want to think of it. But there we were. I supposed, looking back at the years we'd shared, he had been more than a tad unstable. I knew his anger well. I knew how he could twist me up inside and get me to do anything for him. Logan was a fox that knew how to play with mental gymnastics. Every word carried a heavier meaning and you never knew when that bomb would blow up. "I had a dream about him last night. His eyes were hollowed out. There was so much blood on his face. It was really, really fucked. He said it was my fault. I didn't know what he meant at first, then I got the call from his mom." My eyes were fixated at the hardwood floors. They traced the little wood pattern as I spoke.

"You know it's not your fault, right?" I could feel their arms rubbing along my back. I took a moment to think about what Vic said, pairing it to the dream, to the years, to the abuse. I knew it wasn't my fault, but my brain didn't want to believe that. My body didn't want to feel that. Everything in me wanted to take ownership. Vic pulled my head and stared right into my eyes. "You know it wasn't your fault, rriigghhtt?" they asked again. I looked right back at them. It took another moment to really let the words sink in. When you've been with someone who could control you the way Logan controlled me, it became hard to kill habits.

"Right," I said exhaustively. I pulled their slender body close to mine, pink fluff blowing into the air as they fell into my lap. I kissed Vic's cheek, wanting to cry. I wanted to shed every tear I had never shed before. I wanted to make my body a drought of grief, releasing every ounce of feeling in me.

"I'm going to say something." Vic's voice turned serious. "You know I care about you, and you know I've watched as you hurt in your last relationship. I know it was tough, and I know you probably have the urge to go. I don't want to stop you from going, but it is kind of co-dependent to go. You're free; you don't owe the family anything anymore. I'll stay right beside you, but I think going would bring a toxic air because of your history with Logan and his abuse." Vic pulled me close as they finished. Their head nuzzled right into my chest and I kissed them on their forehead.

There was a feeling down in my belly, a feeling that knew they were right. But I knew myself; I knew where I was headed. I cuddled them close, licked up their neck and whispered, "Thank you, babe." We let the sun trail over our bodies, creating blends of pink and gold hue in our living room. I'd never realized how bright we were when we were together, but damn, did I love it.

I hated flying. I hated everything about flying. The minute I walked into an airport my brain was flooded with high-alert questions that almost always remained unanswered. *What if I miss my flight? What if I'm delayed? What if security is taking forever? Do I have enough time?* Every one of those had a simple answer to them, but my brain remained on constant alert. That's anxiety for you.

I was sitting in this plane, waiting for the captain to say something. Anything. I just wanted to be in the air. The earlier my brain knew we were off the ground, the easier it was for me to calm down. I was never afraid of the plane crashing, but goddamn did I hate wondering if my flight would cancel.

Vic was stroking my arm next to me, their thin fingers playing with the fur standing up on my wrist. "You're way too tense, you know that?"

"Aren't I always tense?" I responded. I thought I was being witty at first, but Vic's face showed slivers of agreement with me. I coughed quickly. "I loathe flying."

Vic shook their head, then grabbed my hand and placed

it on their thigh. "With your luck, I understand why. Relax; we got a couple of hours before we arrive south. If you're good, you can tease me." They leaned against me and kissed my neck. I would have said something, but there was hardly anyone on the flight. Late night flights rarely had travelers on it, and quiet travels were what I enjoyed best.

I leaned my seat back slightly and rested my head on Vic's shoulder. "Hey, I'm not a pillow, you know." I rubbed my hand along their thigh and sighed heavily.

"We've been over this. You may not be *a* pillow, but you're definitely *my* pillow. It's in the contract!" I let the ooze out as I fell asleep. Vic replied something, but I passed out hard before I could hear what the raccoon said. They were merely a muffled voice in a sea of darkness, the noise you heard right before you were consumed by slumber.

The moment my eyes were shut, I started to drift. I became lost like Odysseus, knowing my goal was to get home, but to get there I would be forced to confront what dreams came from the currents of my subconscious.

I hated dreaming. On a good day, I would wake up and forget any of that ever happened. But there were always those that stuck with you. Like cigarette burns on your fur. You just couldn't get rid of them. They scarred. They lingered with you. They were a haunting only the body understood, forcing the mind to decipher the message.

In one flick of a switch I was no longer a traveler. I was in my bed. I tried moving my arms, but I couldn't, as if I were paralyzed. I wondered if sleep paralysis could affect your dreams as well, but Vic entered the room. I stared at them for a moment, but then they crawled onto the mattress. It was weird as their clothes seemed to fall off like leaves in the wind. Within that moment, their naked body hovered over mine, their eyes distant, as if hypnotized as they leaned and started sucking on my neck. My first instinct was to rub my hand along their back, but I still couldn't move. I could feel their hand rubbing my cock causing it to rise firmly against their body. They were a flurry of pink, as if cherry blossoms bloomed over their body and engulfed every bit of mine.

They positioned themselves quickly, this barrage of fuchsia moving around in the darkness, their ass moved to my shaft, their back turned to me. I could see them staring back at me as they lowered themselves. I could feel myself enter my lover, the bed creaking with each slide along my shaft. Like turbulence, the bed started to shake. Vic's body grew faster with each passing moment we were together.

I started to forget I was in a dream. I wanted to move. Panic was setting into my chest as I tried to lift my arms, but I could do nothing as they rode me harder and faster.

"B-babe. I c-can't..." Before I could finish the statement, I watched as their body stretched, their back bending backwards and their head meeting mine.

"He'll always be the death of us." The words growled from their mouth. Guttural groans poured out as they rode me hard, their head swirling slowly to meet my own eyes.

"Stop it. Stop it. Stop it..." I said over and over, hoping they'd hear, but there was no sign of that madness ending. I could feel my fingers finally moving. I forced all of my being into trying to get them to lift my hand and arm, but they were barely wiggling on the bed. Out of the darkness, I saw a limb-like arm rotating backwards, claws extended as they reached for my face. Before they could cover my eyes, I could feel the plane moving. I shot my head up quickly and stared around the airplane, seeing all that was around me.

"Yo, you ok? You were shaking pretty bad there, babe. Also, you snore like a motherfucker." They were staring at me with this blend of concern and horrified. As if to say, "I want to help you with whatever just happened, but damn do your snores piss me off."

I slowly calmed down, my heart beat pounding hard against my rib cage. I let my eyes roam around the cabin one last time before I relaxed in my seat. "I'm fine. I just had a weird dream."

You never realize it at first, but the skies are different in every state. The Texas sky was full of blue, its arms wide open as if to welcome you to death. At least that's what I saw the moment I got off the plane that morning. But that was how it was, right? Texas was Texas, a big-ass state with welcoming arms that lay the moment they opened.

I was always on guard in the south. I loathed being there. Even when he was dead, I could still feel some semblance of him in the air. It was suffocating, just like he had been.

We approached the church where the viewing was starting. Vic stood close to me as we walked up to the door. The sky was still as blue, still as welcoming. The sun would go down in a couple hours, but the light needed to show off the state that claimed to be the biggest, as if it were a dick measuring contest.

"You know you're really fuckin' stupid, Axel." I could hear him in the air, or maybe that wasn't him. I didn't know; I couldn't tell.

"What?" I said, looking at Vic. He looked back.

"I didn't say anything," they said while shrugging.

"Stupid. Stupid. Stupid." I started breathing faster; it was as if panic was setting into my chest. I wanted to run. I wanted to escape. The voice was in the wind. It was in the air. He wasn't going to leave me alone, was he? Even in death, he was still going to get into my skin.

"Babe." Vic's hand rubbed along my fur, their pink meshing with my gold. "You okay?" they asked as they huddled close to me.

"Um, yes. I mean, I don't know. Mostly. It's hitting me all

at once," I said, looking at the ground. I could feel my body weakening at the doors of the church.

"Do you even want to go in?" Vic asked, stopping me before we walked in. "If this is going to hurt you, we probably shouldn't do it."

"Logan was a lot of things to me. Terrorizer. Abuser. Lover. I feel unsafe, but I worry if I don't see his body, I'll feel that way the rest of my life. I need to see him; I need to see that he's dead before moving onward." Vic remained silent, nodding me into the church. I kissed their cheek as we pushed through the wooden double doors. An air of incense hit me fast, the putrid smell making me nauseous for a moment. I could never understand why churches needed that shit. I looked at Vic and I could tell they weren't happy about the smell either.

There weren't many inside. Most of the faces I didn't know, but I looked for the coffin. I could see his nose peering out from the open casket, bodies spread out in this somber temple. I could hear Melanie wailing at the front. Echoes were a drastic grenade, calming down only to blow up again amidst her tears. The vixen's make-up was running; I could see it from there. Her hair was thrown about, her clothes partially neat. She was an organized mess, keeping the appearance of grief while managing her own image in front of the few people who attended.

I ran my hands through my mane and tried to soothe the anxiety flowing through my body. "Let's do this," I said lowly, ushering us both to the front of the church. As we neared, it felt like everything around me was washing away. It felt like the world was becoming a blur and all I could see was the coffin and the body. Voices became muffled, a simple echoing noise bouncing in an atmosphere of grief and anger.

The moment we made it to the body, I felt nothing else. Vic wasn't beside me. Melanie wasn't wailing hard in the background. It was just me and the dead before me. I kept my distance from him. I didn't want to touch the coffin, or his body. I just needed to know if he was really dead. Everyone said the dead seemed at peace, but I wondered what he really felt as his body was worked on. Peace was only made when the funeral home took over. Was he afraid? Angry? Or was he just ready to be released from it all?

His auburn fur seemed paler than I last saw him, but embers usually grow weak when ready for death. His hair still flowed down to his shoulders, just like I remembered him. When he would get mad, the strands would separate as if tiny whips were forming from his skull. I wasn't used to seeing him without some disdain on his face.

"I hope you rot." The anger was getting to me then. I had spent years of suffering while sleeping next to him, and I'd swore I'd never see him again. Yet there I was. *Good call, Logan. I guess you got us to see each other once more. Well, I hope this'll be the last.*

I could feel my body tense hard. I wanted to burn the body, wanted to set fire to the whole building in hopes everything and everyone connected to this dead son of a bitch would vanish.

"Now, now, let's not get too hasty. We had good times, didn't we?" My face contorted when I heard his voice. When he rose from the coffin, I became afraid of everything. Would he be haunting me for the rest of my life? Afterlife? Would he not just die and leave me alone? "You were always easy to keep under control." He kept his eyes shut, extending his arm towards me. His fingers were grabbing at air. "Come closer; it's been ages since I felt you. It's not like I can see." His fingers brushed my shirt, causing me to jump back. "You're always welcome here in the valley of the damned. Oh, the times we'll have. You just have to join me. Leave that pathetic excuse for a lover and join me. You know I've always been better. Better at everything."

"I—I don't think..." I started, but he waved a hand to cut me off.

"Don't fucking speak. Just join me. You know you've always loved me. Who else can put you in your place like I do?" His body thrust out from the coffin, trying to grab me. It missed me at first, then his fingers grazed the buttons on my shirt. "You'll be with me soon, you fucking slut!"

"Fuck." I damn near shouted as I stepped far away from the coffin. And in that moment, the world came back. The church, Vic, everyone was staring at me as if I had just ruined the whole ceremony. There was an air in the silence, a stench of anger from every person around me. I wanted nothing more than to run out of the place, hop back onto a plane and never see the Texas blue again. But I was frozen. Frozen by their faces, by their anger.

"It's frightening, isn't it?" Someone spoke from the back. "We all imagine seeing the dead in their best image, but even in death he still looks haunted." A slender coyote approached from the entrance of the church. I didn't recognize him, but he seemed as if he were in worse mourning than Melanie. How did you out-mourn a mother? Or how did you fake your grief? Or maybe I was just reading too much into it.

The coyote took a spot at the front, right next to me. He stood as if it were his spot, a spot just waiting for him as he took the attention of the crowd, his brown fur shown dark underneath the dim lighting of this church. It was weird. As I stared at him, I noticed his fur stiffened as if he were frightened or angry at being there, but ready to handle any group that sat in front of him. His eyes narrowed at me before he began speaking up. He had a slow gaze as he stared at me, then Vic.

"Seeing the body of a loved one is always frightening. It's a reminder that time on this planet is limited for all of us.

And though my boyfriend left us sooner than we imagined, nobody escapes death's hands. And nobody escapes the cruelty of this world. I know eulogies are saved for the final funeral, but as someone who loved him wholly and unconditionally, I cannot keep silent. Logan touched us all. Let us remember that as we see him lying before us. Without life." The coyote adjusted his tie, then turned to me and extended his hand. "I'm Tom. You must be Axel; Logan has talked about you before." His face wore sympathy, but there was something there behind it. As if he were wearing a mask and beneath the mask he was plotting.

"I'm sorry we had to meet under these circumstances," I responded. Vic wrapped their arm around mine and huddled close to me.

"We should probably get going," Vic chimed in swiftly. I could feel the tension in their body, feel their fear. And for a brief moment, I started to feel it, too.

"We'll have to have dinner some time. I'm sure Melanie would love to have us over for a quiet evening. You and I both knew Logan well, and she's always talked about how much she loved you." Tom was pushing hard now.

"We'll have to take you up on that, but we really have to go now. We've had a long flight and I would like to get some rest," I said sternly. The more Vic clung to me, the more I worried for us both. Tom looked back at Logan's mom, then to us and gave a small wave.

"I'll talk to Melanie and see what we can set up."

Vic and I walked swiftly to the head of the church. The moment we pushed through the double doors and into the open air, I felt my heart sink to my stomach. "I don't know what happened in there, but it freaked me the fuck out," I said looking at my partner.

The raccoon pulled me in and kissed my cheek. "Should we even go to the funeral tomorrow? You freaked out in the church and I don't want you to over extend yourself."

"I don't know. Let's get back to the hotel and rest. We'll play it by ear," I said as I started to calm down. Vic took the keys from me. We hopped in the car and drove fast down the highway, away from the church. Away from Tom. Just away.

The moon was full that night. I sat by the window of our room and just watched it. I had it propped open so the smoke would escape as I took hits off my vape. I was still on edge from the viewing. What was I seeing? What had I been seeing that whole time? How much of my mind was I losing? I knew I was going mad. I felt it in my body. I felt the constant panic seizing my body every day. My nightmares, my visions, the feelings I got around people. I was starting to feel no one was safe except for Vic.

There I was in old territory then. A land familiar, yet unfamiliar at the same time. So much of that state looked different since I'd last seen it, but the sky looked the same— empty save for the moon.

There was a small breeze out that night, yet it wasn't soothing. There was an eeriness it held as it travelled through; a sense of dread filling the atmosphere around us. Almost like a warning. Almost like the air was saying "something wicked comes this way." But what was wicked versus what was madness was something I wasn't able to differentiate. The lines were blurring for me. My descent into that crippling insanity felt as if it was happening rapidly. I wanted to crawl out from it, but I feared I was sinking to a depth I wouldn't be able to return from.

"You haven't vaped in years, love." Caught red handed.

"I know you don't like it. I'm sorry." Though I wanted to push myself away from them, I turned to face them. My eyes filling with tears now, I could feel the wind pick up. It was a rough breeze trailing through the back of my mane as

I faced my lover. They nodded their head upward, as if to say "What's going on?" And I fell to the floor, tears streaming from my eyes.

"I thought I could handle this," I said, amidst sobs. "He has been tormenting me ever since he died, like some kind of haunted beast from beyond. I thought I saw him move at the viewing. I've had nightmares. I think I'm going crazy. You see that, right?" I looked at them, begging for something, anything to make the madness end. The raccoon took my hand and pulled me into them. They kissed my cheek and I collapsed against their body, just sobbing. What else could I do? What else was there to do? I cried more than I ever had before. "I'm afraid," I whispered into their ear. "So, so afraid."

They rubbed their hand along my back and pulled me into bed. "We'll tackle whatever it is together, love. Anything that comes at us, we'll tackle it together." They kissed me, pulled the covers over us and just let me cry the rest of the night. Their arms wrapped tightly around me as I started to calm down.

"You remember when we went skinny dipping, and you didn't know how to swim? You were so scared to even touch the water. Although I've always heard cats hate water, even the big bulky ones like you. It was the hottest of all the days we've been together. I was already swimming around and you had just taken off your trunks. I just about drowned the moment you got naked, not used to seeing pure hotness in front of me." Vic spoke in a whisper. I kept my eyes closed. I could see the lake, the scattered green around us separated by twigs, dirt and whatever trash was left by previous visitors. "When you saw me sinking into the water, you jumped right in. If you didn't know how to swim before, you knew right then. I love you, Axel. I don't understand it all, and I can't know what you're going through. But I'm jumping in. I'm jumping into the deepest part of this with you." They kissed the back of my neck. It wasn't long before we both fell asleep.

I kept Vic close the whole night. I didn't want to let them go; I didn't want to let anything go. I was losing parts of myself. Each time I saw Logan, I felt as if I went deeper into madness. I felt as if he were pushing me to do the same. He'd never wanted to let me go, but how often do abusers move on from the ones they control? Even in death you weren't safe.

The moon was still bright outside. Though I yearned for another smoke to calm my nerves, I didn't want to leave the bed. I didn't want to leave Vic. I wanted to feel as safe as possible and that was there. With them. Safe is that bed. Safe was being in their arms. Safe was not being on the floor or by the window or staring at your phone. Safe was there. In that moment. And I felt like it was one of the few moments I'd have in life where I'd feel completely safe.

I looked at the clock. 3:00 a.m. There wasn't going to be any sleep tonight, was there? Seemed insomnia had doomed me for the night. I tried to keep my body still, staring at the red lines of the digital alarm clock. It was the only thing lit up in our room. Until my phone buzzed. A flash lit up the table around it. It was the loudest buzz in our room. Everything else remained still, remained silent. I needed silence. I knew nothing would be there in that darkness if everything was still silent.

The moment I thought of reaching for my phone, I heard it. The door banged briefly. Three knocks. Three short, loud knocks.

I didn't answer. I stayed still on our bed.

Three more knocks.

"Oooohhhh Aaaaxxeeellllll. Come out to plaaayyyy." I heard him. His nasal, deviant voice echoed outside of the door.

"Leave me alone!" I shouted. I didn't care if I woke Vic

then; Logan needed to stop.

"Bitch, don't tell me what to do!" His voice raged, turning to a grunting angry mess. "I'm coming for you, Axel. I'm coming fast, and your stupid ass better be ready." An auburn smoke oozed from the bottom of the door. The room was almost filled with it after a few moments. I shook Vic to wake them, but they didn't respond. I slapped them. No response, so I tried to carry them. Carry them off that bed, but where would we go? The moment my feet touched the ground we would have to bolt through the door, but the fox was there.

So I waited. I waited for him to appear. Waited for his figure to form before me. What else could I do in that small room? The window was stories up.

Though it took forever, Logan finally appeared through the red smoke. His eyes were gone. Like they were in my first dream. He stood in the moonlight, arms crossed. I could feel him staring at me, yet every time he appeared before me, he was blind. I held Vic close. I held him hard against me as I trembled before that ghost.

"It's been a while, Axe." Logan's voice was cold. There was a gruffness in his throat I hadn't heard before. I wondered if the nature of his death had changed his voice, added the raspy nature to it, as I had never heard him like that. It was sinister. It was something I wanted to never hear again. Granted, I didn't want to ever hear Logan's voice anyway, but never like that. Fear crept over my body.

"Why can't you just leave me alone?" I said in near sobs.

"I wouldn't be dead if it weren't for you," he responded, his hand thrusting outward to point at me.

"What did I do? I didn't force you to make the choice you did. I didn't whisper in your ear to kill yourself, Logan." I was near shouting now. Vic still in my arms, my voice kept getting louder the more I talked.

"There's one way to get rid of me, Axe. You just have to

cross over," he said as he waved his hand over the mattress, causing a noose to appear before me. "I'll leave you little bitch lover alone if you do."

I looked down at the noose. Then at Vic. The possibility of ending all that started to creep into my mind. If it meant saving Vic, I was almost crazy enough to do it. I started to reach for it. I could see him lean forward with anticipation. Whispers hovered around me as he waited. "Do it. Do it. Do it," flooded the air over and over. It was like a medley of temptation, pushing me to end everything. Then I stopped.

"Why do you say it was my fault?" I asked him. He grew impatient. I could see his fists balling up as if he were ready to hit me.

"Because you left me. I told you what I'd do. I told you if you left I would kill myself." His fur started to produce a crimson smoke much like the smoke he used to enter our room.

"Your death isn't my fault. You made a choice. I had to leave, Logan."

"No!" His fist struck the bed. "You couldn't leave! I owned you. I was your boyfriend. We made promises to stay with each other. You were mine, you filthy fuckin' bitch!" He started to crawl onto our mattress. At that moment, I grabbed Vic and flew off the bed. We rolled onto the floor and I picked them up, carrying them around to the door but stopped by the smoke.

I knew I would have to cross over. I knew I would have to jump through the crimson smoke to escape. That didn't make it any less horrifying for me. "Fuck it," I exclaimed and made a jump. As I made through the other side, something grabbed me. Vic flew out of my arms and I tripped on the floor. The smoke was pulling me back in. My lover's body inches away from me, the fuchsia raccoon lying on the floor, I called out to them. "Vic!" I shouted.

No response.

"Vic!" I shouted again, this time longer.

Still nothing. My ankles were enveloped by Logan's presence. I saw him crawl off the bed and position himself at my feet. He had this way of making the smoke move as he moved. It was attached to him, attached to his movements. I felt his hands wrap around my feet and when I looked down, his face stretched wide as he held my feet to his tongue. He let out a rough laugh as he licked through my toes, then started to swallow me.

The further I dropped into the crimson, the less I saw of my partner. I could barely make the outline of their slender body. "I love you," I yelled as they were just out of sight. Dark red enveloped everything as I descended into the belly of the fox. The monster had gotten me. I felt like I was falling. As if this body I entered was nothing more than a void that wouldn't end. Wind rushed through my mane, my fur; I wondered what would happen the moment I hit the floor. I screamed, begged, pleaded. Anything to get out of that madness. Anything to be free, but there was nothing coming for me. I was stuck there, falling for what seemed like an eternity.

What else was left for me then? I fell farther, the wind getting stronger, as if I were becoming weightless the more I dropped. I looked down, or what I thought was down. Everything was black around me, until I looked and saw something coming right for me. I couldn't make it out at first, then my eyes adjusted and it got clearer. I could see the grass coming for me. I could see a field below. I was almost there. I could almost reach it. I thrust out my arms, anticipating my fall to break every bone in my body. I didn't care if I died then. I had nothing else. Logan had taken it all from me and forced me there, forced me into that falling prison.

I reached out, and the moment I could touch it, I thrust

up and was back at the hotel. Vic was standing over me, shaking my body. I didn't know what to say, so I just pulled them in and hugged them harder than I ever had before.

"I thought you were about to die," they said. "You were shaking so hard, mumbling words I couldn't understand." I could see tears forming in their eyes. "I thought you was gonna die, babe. I didn't know what to do." They collapsed against my body.

I told them everything I dreamt. Both of us were shaken, unsettled. We didn't want to see the outside world. Didn't want to leave our room. Not for a moment. We just wanted each other.

We didn't go to his funeral.

His mom was calling. I watched the phone buzz for over five minutes. She wasn't taking no for an answer that time. On its millionth ring I picked up. "Hi, Melanie!" I tried to say as nicely as possible.

"You weren't there!" she screamed at me. "You weren't at his funeral! How could you do that to my fucking son!" She continued for what seemed like forever, but I understood the gist of it.

"Melanie, I was able to make it to the viewing and pay my respects then. The service was not something I was able to get to. I'm sorry if—"

"Oh, fuck you, Axel. You ain't done anything for him since y'all split. And to think he loved you." I was getting pissed off now. That bitch had the audacity to call me up and shame me for not attending her abusive son's funeral?

"Well little Miss Don't Fuck With Me, Logan was a monster. An abusive fucking monster. And to think you gave birth to that thing," I responded and hung up immediately. I was shaking with anger the moment I got off the phone. I wanted to break every window in our hotel room. I wanted to go out and destroy every car in the parking lot. I wanted Poseidon to destroy the earth with floods.

I wanted to be left alone. I wanted the world to just take its grasp on me and let me go for one day. I wanted just love and to live in that love.

I wanted my past gone.

I looked over to Vic, who was resting their eyes on our bed. We hadn't left the hotel since the viewing. "Babe, let's go out."

They slowly opened their eyes, their slender body rising with a large breath. The raccoon brushed their hand down their chest, then stretched themselves out before rising. "Out where?" they asked flatly. Their face wore a bit of concern as their eyes studied me.

"Anywhere, really. I'm starting to feel a little crazy here. Some air will help." I was still shaken by the phone call with Melanie. My hands were quaking as he stared out of the window. "When I lived here, there was a beach not far. The water is murky as shit, but I always like to feel the sand between my toes. Let's go there."

Vic rolled off the bed, their briefs sliding off their waste as they landed on the floor. They adjusted themselves and wrapped their arms around me. "Then let's get out of here." They kissed my neck and held me tight. I put a hand on their arms. I didn't want them to let go. I didn't know what would happen to me if they did. I started to feel like what was real and what was dream was merging too much for me. When they started to unravel behind me, I turned around and kissed their belly, then got up to get dressed.

The hotel phone started to ring. I answered that promptly. "Hello?" I knew I was rude at the start, so I cleared my throat, trying to adjust myself.

"There's someone here to see you? They said y'all met at a

funeral." I rolled my eyes.

"I'll be right down." I didn't waste any time. Vic was still getting ready and I just flew out of the room. Fortunately, I had some pants on. My feet were swift, carrying me down the hall and though I thought of using the elevator, I opted for running down the stairs, which honestly felt quicker. Most would argue, but that didn't matter. The moment I walked into the lobby, I saw him there. Fucking Tom.

"Axel!" he said in that loud Texas accent. "We missed you at the funeral yesterday. What happened?"

I took in a deep breath and tried to compose myself. "Tom, it's great to see you. It's been years since I'd been in Texas and I wanted to show Vic around. Texas is kind of a home to me."

Tom's face contorted. "So, you missed Logan's funeral?"

"I paid my respects the other day. The service isn't a requirement," I responded quickly.

He shrugged. "As long as you got a clean conscience. I guess that's all that matters."

I was furious now. I could feel steam rising from my fur. My fists were clenched, my teeth were grinding. I was ready to kill that fucker in front of me. Ready to drown him in every ocean on the planet. "You should probably go now, Tom."

His smile grew wide when I told him that. "Did you see him last night?"

"What do you me—"

"He's coming for you, Axe. He's coming to take you to hell with him. I don't know why he couldn't let you go, but he can't. Almost makes me just a tad jealous. If he wasn't a bastard." He started to walk away.

"Why? Why are you helping him?" I asked, still fuming with anger beneath my fur.

"You don't just deny Logan. He's like the devil. When he

bothers you, he won't go away."

I felt a hand on my shoulder. "You need to leave." I turned around and Vic was standing there. I saw their fists clenched, ready to throw the first punch.

Tom put his hands up and backed away. "I'm not lookin' to get into a fight there." I could see him trying to read my partner. He studied their body vigorously with his eyes as he continued to back away. "I'm only here to deliver a message. Logan will return. And he will have you."

"Fuck off," I shouted at him. I was ready to fight as well. He jumped back and started to walk briskly to the door. Vic grabbed my hand and looked at me as if to ask if I were alright. I only nodded.

"Let's get out of here," I said as we waited for Tom to leave.

We walked barefoot in the sand. As I looked around at the beach, I couldn't help but think it was just like I remembered it. Dirty. Trashy. Broken. Much like myself. The waves flooded our feet as we walked the shoreline. I saw Vic staring at the water, and I knew what they were thinking. *Yes, little raccoon, my home is a mess.* That was most of our memories, right? We held them close to us as if they were our children. We held them as if they were biblical, but there was always a crack we never saw, or failed to see at first. Some things took time to spread evenly in our minds; others were quick to show themselves.

"The water seems...really filthy," the raccoon said as they eyed the waves coming towards us.

They weren't wrong. The gulf had never actually been that great of a beach, but as a kid it was all I had. "It's been that way ever since I remember it. It's disgusting looking. I probably shouldn't have swum in it as a child, but what did I know, right?" Vic pushed my arm.

"Well, I hope you have standards now," they teased.

"I know you call it home, but let's be real. This place is a hellhole."

It had been years since I stepped foot on Texas soil, and though the heat was welcoming enough, I couldn't wait to get out.

As we came up to a food shack that was closed, I saw him. That motherfucker, Tom. My gut was telling me to run; to take Vic and get out, but we kept going. I wondered if Vic had seen him, too, but it didn't appear so. They were still staring at the water. As we got closer, I shouted out, "Following us, I see."

Tom didn't say anything as he stood up to greet us. At least that was what I thought. The moment he stood, I saw him pull a gun from his waste. He pointed it at us and I pulled Vic with me to the side. "What the—" I heard them exclaim, but there wasn't time to explain. I heard a gunshot. Two. Three.

Vic and I ran, then I heard them scream. We both plummeted to the sand. I raised myself quickly and tried to see what happened, and then I saw it. A bullet had hit them right in their thigh. I pressed my hands firmly on it to try and stop the bleeding. "Someone call for help! Please!" I shouted, but there was no one around. The beach was empty. I guessed Vic and I hadn't noticed how secluded we were in the open ocean breeze. I didn't have much time before Tom caught up with us. The coyote was running fast as I held firm on my raccoon's wound. All I saw was this beastly canine, teeth gritting, lips wide, eyes wild. The man that stood before us was out for blood. He had been stalking us every step of the way. From the viewing, to the hotel, to there. Tom was just a few steps behind us most of the time.

"Wh—" Tom threw his fist into my face, and I was out before I could ask.

"Looks like he finally got you, Axe," I heard in the darkness. I couldn't see anything. I could feel my head twist around, but my sight was all gone.

"What the fuck!" I screamed out, but it was like screaming into the void.

I waited in the silence, my heart raging against my chest as I tried to see around me. I wanted something, anything to come before me, but I was left with darkness. As I started to resolve myself and calm down, the void erupted with laughter. I was pummeled with his insidious voice from all sides.

"You have no idea what's coming, Axe. You'll join me soon!" The words poured out amidst his erupting cackles. "But for that, you must wake up."

"What?" I said, trying to understand the madness encircling me.

"Wake the fuck up!" I felt something hit my face and slowly I started to see again. I awoke to sickly blue walls. Or were they green? I couldn't tell, but I knew whoever chose that paint was a failure at design and probably should have been fired from cannon. Either way, the moment I saw those walls, I knew I was in her house. Fucking Melanie.

"Well, looks like the brave lion has finally woken up. Took you long enough." Tom sat across from me, a leg propped up on the table.

"You fuckin' piece of shit!.." I tried to get up, but I was bound to that shitty flowery chair. Immediately Vic's words flooded my head. Immediately I started to regret ever coming back to Texas. Now there we were. I stared down at the yellow flowers between my legs, and although it took me a moment to realize, I immediately grew angry when I saw I was naked. "What the fuck are you doing to me?" I roared, raging harder against the chair.

"Settle the fuck down." He put his gun against my chest. "We're not done. See, Logan wanted us to do something for him, should he ever die."

"I don't want anything from that fucking lunatic! He's been stalking me for days. I just want to be left the fuck alone!"

The coyote got right up into my face, hand against my throat. How he found it underneath my mane, I'm not sure, but he held me firm. The gun got tighter against my chest each moment he held it against me. "Shut the fuck up! He always talked about you, even when we were together. God, I hated hearing him say your name. And here we are. Are you happy, Logan? I coulda killed him myself if I'd known this was gonna happen." The coyote was raging hard in the home. He slammed his fist down on the table, arms shaking in his anger.

Melanie stayed in the kitchen. She smoked a cigarette as she stirred a pot. Though it smelled good, I was not in the mood for any of her cooking. I looked over to her and nodded. "And what does Melanie think of all this? Surely she doesn't want me in her home, nor my partner."

She took a long drag from her cigarette then turned to look at me. "Boy, I'm merely the cook in all this. I never quite approved of Logan's affairs, but since it's my son's last wish, I saw this through."

Tom shook his head and walked up to her. "You're more than just a cook. Remember what you did?"

"What did she do, Tom?" I asked quickly.

He turned around and punched me in the face. I'd always hated how small the kitchen was in that home. "Shut up. You'll see soon."

"Why make him wait any longer, Tom?" My heart dropped. I knew that voice. I knew it was him. I knew that fox was somewhere in the house even though I'd seen the body a couple days back. I knew he was there. I started to search around the room. I wanted to see. I wanted to see him in front of me.

Footsteps approached. They were like a slow beating heart thumping across hardwood floors. I felt like this was taking longer than it should have, but Logan always focused on making his entrance perfect.

However, Logan didn't show.

A flurry of pink walked past me. I saw their body. They stood tall, as if their spine had grown in length since I last saw them. I couldn't understand what I was seeing before me. Though it looked like the lover I'd known, there was something different about them. That wasn't Vic. That was far from Vic.

The raccoon took a seat as Melanie set the table. Strands of her blonde hair brushed against me as dinner was placed before us all. Vic's body took a look at me, eyes studying every inch of my face before they started to speak. "You could never escape me, Axe."

My fur stood on edge. My mane stiffened as my eyes widened. That was not Vic's voice. "L-Logan?" I couldn't keep the fear out of my voice. I couldn't comprehend what was happening there. Why did my partner sound like my ex? I started to hyperventilate, but Vic's fist slowed my breathing when they slammed it on the table.

"Well, I'm not your stupid fuck of a partner. But Vic was a convenient body. I just inched my way as any fox does." Melanie started filling plates with side dishes. Mac and Cheese, mashed potatoes. They had always been Logan's favorite. He never ate anything green. Couldn't even get a vegetable down without gagging on it as if he'd taken a big ass dick. But that had been him. Or was him. I didn't know anymore. Logan's eyes settled on the dish in the middle. I saw the raccoon's arms stretch into the center. "Let's reveal the main course, mother. I'm sure we're all dying to see it." I hated Logan's voice. I hated how he possessed my partner. I wondered if Vic would even be able to return to their body or if they were lost to the afterlife.

I wanted to mourn. I wanted to shed every ounce of liquid in my body as I cried for him. But I couldn't cry. Logan hated crying. I watched as Melanie revealed the main course, and what I saw made me sick. Logan's head sat on a platter in the middle of the table. Slices of meat were placed decoratively around it.

"What the fuck? What the fucking fuck?" I shouted. I didn't want to believe anything before my eyes.

Logan pounded on the table again. "Shut the fuck up!" His voice was booming. He ensured that he would be the dominant force in the room. "I bet you were wondering what my mother was placing before us. Fox, it's what's for dinner! My body lies before us, though in pieces and cooked in a delectable chicken broth, I'm sure. Think of this like chicken and dumplings. Remember how you used to fuck it up when we were together? Well, take a bite. See how easy it is to make."

I was not going to eat that. I just sat and stared at the contents in front of me. Tom started chanting the more time passed. "Take a bite. Take a bite. Take a bite," over and over. The more he did it, the louder it got and the more maddening it became. I watched as all sense of sanity left his body. He grabbed a fistful of our meal and stuffed it in his mouth. "Take a bite. Take a bite." Chunks and bits spewed everywhere before us. I almost threw up when it hit me in the face.

"I'm not eating that shit," I said plainly, trying not to mourn the site in front of me. I was shaking, every inch of me was shaking. I wanted to roar out and kill the trio before me. And though I knew it was Vic's body, a part of me believed they weren't coming back. My body was consumed by rage. Underneath, my gold fur was embers waiting to be unleashed upon them.

That angered the coyote even more. He took another fistful and rubbed the food all over my face. I felt thick, mucus-like gobs becoming embedded into my mane and my fur. Then I tasted it. I tasted Logan's flesh. And it disgusted me. I felt sick. I felt angered. I was shaking with rage the moment that shit hit my tongue.

I struggled wildly against Tom, eventually headbutting him, which threw him back against the table. I could feel my hands becoming loose underneath the bindings. The family was not good at keeping anything secure. The ropes fell from my wrists, and the moment Tom got up to punch me, I drove my fist into his face. Without hesitation, I grabbed my fork and jabbed it hard into his eye. I dug the metal object in as far as I could before digging it out and tossing it aside. I took my claws and dug them into his throat, ripping off bits of flesh and fur when I pulled my hand back. "You motherfucker!" I raged, slashing and digging and slashing into the coyote beneath me. I started to expose everything that lay beneath his skin. He jumped up and tried to bite me in a flash, but I forced my paws between his jaw. His teeth sank into my fingers, but I kept at him, keeping his jaw open and stretching it until I heard it crack and pop. When I broke his jaw, I threw his head to the floor and started to choke him. My claws were shoved far beneath the skin of his neck. I wanted to feel his life come out of him. I wanted to see his last eye drain. I wanted to hear the final breath as I killed the son of a bitch.

And then he died.

I turned around to find the family still sitting at the table. Melanie as stone faced as ever, and Logan watching from afar. "I didn't really like Tom that much, anyways. He was fun to play with, but nothing like you, Axe."

"Fuck you!" I responded, taking a plate and throwing

it hard at the raccoon's face. It pained me to do it, to do anything that could hurt Vic, but if Logan was inside that body, I didn't think Vic would ever be returning. "They aren't coming back, are they?" I finally got the courage to ask.

Logan stared at his fingernails. "No, I don't suppose your little fuck adventure will be returning. We needed an empty body and the only way to do that is to, well, kill a person. It's a very daunting and long drawn-out task. I won't bore you with the details, but my mother is just a doll when it comes to bringing the dead back to life."

I roared and threw another plate. This time I took Melanie by her hair and wrapped my hands around her throat. "I'll fucking kill her, Logan. End whatever it is you're doing. End it now."

"My mother is already dead, dear. Seems she ate a bite while you and Tom were fighting, though Tom would have died eventually. My mother laced your meals with cyanide, so even you will die at some point. You were all going to die. My body is what will kill you. It's what Jesus should have done for his followers. He just wasn't as creative as I am."

I tried to understand what Logan was saying. "We're not your followers, Logan!"

"I know that. Doesn't mean I can't bring people with me into the afterlife. Loneliness is a tiresome feeling, and I'm fabulous enough for an entourage." I was getting annoyed. I still carried rage within me and hearing Logan's words only made the fires that much stronger.

"You could never let me go, could you, Logan?" I finally asked.

I watched as eyes stared right into me. All I wanted was to have Vic back, to hold their body in mine, but Vic was gone and that bastard fox had taken over their body. "Eat of my flesh, Axel. I've got so much planned for you where we're going." I saw the crimson smoke again. It slowly escaped from

Vic's body, first through their mouth, then their eyes, then all over. I knew what would happen if I got caught in the smoke. I knew I would die. I knew what I would see. "Eat of my flesh," Logan said again, this time his voice growing darker. I hated when he used that voice. Even when he was alive, I knew I was in trouble when he sounded like a demon. Some days I'd referred to him as the demon fox to my friends; then there we were.

I thought of running. I knew I didn't want to be enveloped by the smoke, but the fires within me raged and I couldn't stop myself. I leapt forward and grabbed Logan by the neck. It felt satisfying to be the one to pin him against a wall. Memories of the fox beating me, calling me stupid, worthless, saying that I should just kill myself. Everything he ever said and did funneled into my hands as I squeezed his throat tightly. I could see him try to speak, but I wasn't letting him. I drove a fist into his face as the smoke started to envelope us both. I wasn't going to get taken without a fight. "I'll fucking kill you! I'll send you back to whatever hell you came from, you sonofabitch!" I continued squeezing, everything inside me aflame, raging against the demon that'd been plaguing my days.

Suddenly, I heard someone bust through the door. "Get your hands up! Holy fuckin' shit," I heard behind me. I turned around, my hands high in the air.

"He's coming for us. Get out!" I shouted, but before I could get another word, the figure fired its gun. I was pummeled with bullets, my body flailing until I hit the ground.

I couldn't see anything. My vision was gone, but I could still hear. Multiple footsteps ran into the home. Everything inside was just chattering as I tried to make out what they were saying.

All I could hear was, "I think that lion killed them all."

INTERLUDE 4

Like taking a punch to the face, Allen returned to consciousness. He felt the cold air of the stadium whip against his naked body, shaking profusely as his eyes trailed around. He was still bound. The wood of the stockade dug into his hands and neck as he started to thrash against it. Yet he knew he wouldn't escape the bindings that easily; he felt there was nothing else to do. He thrashed harder, trying to break open the frame that held him firmly, until a hand started to trail along his ass. He knew that touch, knew what it meant; who it was from. His eyes fixated on the ram's blue fur as he appeared before him. Taking in a large breath, his nose cringed at the smell of the ram's musk. Pushing his bulge into Allen's face, he started to speak. "We have one more game to play, little wolf."

"P-please. No more games. I just want to go h-home." Allen's voice was starting to lose hope of ever leaving Carnage. His body quaked in the broken stadium, his eyes trying to look away from the ram. He focused hard at the empty bleachers, his fur flying off in the air each second he was locked down.

"There's always a price, wolf. I'm sure you know that. Sure, we can forget the games, and you can walk along your merry way out of here, but that's not what we do here. And I don't plan on letting a fine view just toddle off." The ram caressed Allen's back, sliding his hand down and along his ass. The blue flame pressed his thumb against his prey's hole, forcing the wolf to shiver once pressure was applied. Shame started to bubble up inside of Allen; thoughts of Mike and fears of his disappointment at his current predicament plagued him fiercely, forcing him to shake hard underneath the ram's hand.

"Stop it! Stop touching me!" Allen shouted back. He wished he had the strength to break apart the wooden frame, thrashing against the restraints again.

The ram drove his fist into the wolf's snout. Blood spewed out from Allen's nostrils as he tried to fight. Images of his boyfriend started to rage in his skull. He couldn't bear to see Mike's disappointed eyes, his arms crossed as if to say "I knew you would do this to me." There was a storm raging in his chest; not wanting to see his relationship washed away with jealousy, Allen continued to try and break loose, knowing he wasn't strong enough to break the wood. He thought that maybe if he fought harder, Mike would stay with him. The thought of losing him was fatal. Although his friends tried to warn Allen of Mike's jealous temper, he was already bound. *Who else would love me?* he asked himself. *Who else would see me the way Mike does?*

"Don't speak until I tell you to." His voice commanded the wolf to listen. He drove another fist into his face, then planted his bulge against Allen's muzzle. "You're in my domain, pup. You're not done here until the last game is played." Allen was afraid of what else the blue ram had in store for him. Slowly, he calmed himself down and focused on the gatekeeper's words. "In my hand I hold a deck of tarot cards. I will draw one. If you are able to guess the card hiding underneath, I will let you go. If you do not, you'll remain here as a personal toy for me. To make it fair, I will give you three guesses." The gatekeeper shuffled the cards. Allen could feel his heart leaping out of his chest. He closed his eyes and started whispering to himself.

"I want to go home. I want to go home. I want to go home," he repeated, the words leaving his tongue quaking. Tears started to form in his eyes as the ram started to set out three cards.

He waved his hand and stared at the wolf. "Your first guess."

Allen tried to think, tried to pull anything and everything to find a card. He knew he wasn't a psychic, but there had to at least be some card he could muster in his mind. "There's always a death card. It's shown in movies so much. Death," he said, his voice quivering with each word.

The first card was flipped. "Wrong. It's judgment. Your next guess." The ram spoke flatly. Allen wanted to read the blue flame before him, but he couldn't. The ram remained like stone.

He tried guessing again, thinking of the tales he saw. "Um, The Devil," he spoke again, quivering. He just wanted it all to end; his body felt like the ground in an earthquake, a violent rage of shivering. He felt as if his flesh would tear apart the more he shook.

"Wrong again. The Hanged Man. You have one more guess." The ram removed the two cards and put them back in the deck.

Allen thought for a few moments. "What other cards can there be?" he said aloud.

"I'll need your answer soon. Your time is almost up," the ram spoke flatly.

Allen tried to think of all that had happened to him upon

entering the haunted house. He felt his gut tell him to go with the first card that came to mind and he blurted it out. "The Fool."

The ram flipped over the card and let out an annoyed sigh. "Correct," he said. "And what a fool you are." He leaned in and started to whisper in Allen's ear, a hand trailing down the wolf's back and grabbing his ass. "Mike will only ever see you as a slut. Whatever connection you both share is a thread ready to break, if it hasn't already." He waved his fingers and the stock was lifted. "You are free to leave, but there'll only be another challenge ahead. If you die, your soul will come back here. And I'll be waiting, pup. There's so much I'd like to do to you." The ram licked his lips as he waved his hand again; a crowd of spirits were revealed, all watching from the bleachers as Allen ran out. He ran far, seeing the hallway he entered. He didn't wait for his guide, he just ran.

Mike found himself in the mouth of the bull, as if time stood still while he was out. His body sloshed around on the giant's tongue as he fought to keep from being swallowed. "What the fuck is going on!" he screamed as his hands tried to keep a grip on the bull's teeth. He took his claws and dug them hard across the top of the bull's mouth in hopes of hurting his predator.

The bull roared, his mouth opening wide and emitting a sound that filled the cavern outside. The basset hound grunted hard as hot breath attacked his back, as if flames were touching his ass. He tried to crawl out of the bull's mouth, but the giant grabbed him with his hand and squeezed fervently.

Mike could see the creatures below, all running away. He tried to dig his nails into the bull's hand, but it only made the minotaur squeeze harder.

"Seems there's no escape for you, dear Mike." A voice came from the blackness. The basset hound tried looking around, his cheek flapping as his head turned rapidly.

"Get me out of here!" he cried. The voice only chuckled at the demand.

"What kind of host would I be if I didn't give you a scare?" the voice replied.

"Linus? Get me out of here, now! We didn't sign up for this!" Mike protested.

"Oh, but you did. Carnage is a carnival of horrors. It's customary for some not to leave this home." The bull lifted the basset hound up again. The hand wrapped firmly around Mike's whole body as he brought him to the bull's thick penis. The minotaur roared as he started to insert Mike's body into his urethra, like a living sounding device. Mike fought his way against what was happening, but he wasn't strong enough to push back against the bull's strength. Slowly, he felt his bones become enveloped by the minotaur's cock, his belly pressed down as if a girdle changing his body. Before the basset hound's head was pushed in, he heard Linus speak. "I'll be sure to tell your boyfriend...Allen, was it? I'll tell him you send your love, darling."

The bull started to stroke himself as Mike's whole body was covered in flesh. The hound tried to push and wriggle against every inch of skin that covered him, but with the bull's hand brushing over his body, he couldn't escape his current fate. A free hand rubbing along his torso, the minotaur massaged every inch of his shaft beneath his cave. Linus' laughter bounced between rocky walls and dirt as he watched from afar. Mike knew there was no hope for him then. The bull's hand crushing any bit of bone inside his body, he closed his eyes and waited for the inevitable end to happen. The bull roared once more in the cavern; spires from the ceiling shook as the elongated growl sent the bull's raging cock into climax. Mike's body shot out from the tip along with the minotaur's cum spewing after him. "Fuuuccck..." the phonemes spewed out like a river as his body flew towards the ground, his face planting hard on rough stone surface. The hound's neck broke on impact, blood splattering from his body. Linus watched as he twitched for a few moments, then walked out of the cave.

Rachel flew back from the table. It took a moment for her eyes to adjust to the bar's dim lighting. She looked around the room and noticed all of the dead staring directly at her. Her eyes bolted to the turtle that led her to this table. "Why are they staring at me?"

Her gatekeeper took a shot of his own tears and stretched his neck. "Most of the dead you see here want a life outside of this bar. In order for them to leave they have to learn to let go, but they've started to believe they could leave if they had a living body."

The lioness' eyes widened as she looked around her. "They want to kill me?"

"Well, yes. Your soul would have to leave your body for them to enter," he said, taking another drink. "I'm sure you're wondering now how best to leave this bar." The bartender waded through the sea of spirits as the turtle took another drink of his tears. A knife was set before the pair at the table and the turtle waved him away. "You'll need to leave a piece of yourself. Otherwise, a spirit here will claim your body and try to leave. You will die, and your spirit will remain here with the rest of us."

The lioness didn't know what to do at first. She reached for the knife, her hands shaking at the choice she was being forced to make. Her stomach wrenched as she sat there, staring at the tool she held in her hands.

Fingers from the spirits in the room started to trail over her shoulders. Her beige fur stiffened as she felt them. She could feel their eyes watching her, feel them wishing she wouldn't take the option her turtle gatekeeper bestowed upon her. Her ears perched as she heard their whispers. "Stay with us. Stay. Stay. Stay with us. We are all one here. You don't need to leave us." The voices started getting stronger; their hands started to tug and pull at her quaking body.

She held the knife to her pinky finger, her body keeping her from driving it through her bone. Fighting between her own fear and the voices, she screamed. "Shut the fuck up!" The lioness raised the knife and drove it down hard into her pinky finger. A wealth of pain surged through her body. She screamed louder each time she drove the knife into her finger. She repeated the motion, blood splattering on her face as she continued until the finger was severed from her hand.

She tossed the knife aside and held her hand close to her. Rachel couldn't bear the pain much longer. She writhed in her seat, holding her hand against her belly. The gatekeeper picked up the pinky and examined it for a moment. She was about to say something, but was stopped when he held his hand up.

"I suppose this donation is good enough." A door opened behind the lioness. She was quick to get up, but before she could leave, the turtle stopped her. "This room is not the only horror you'll meet. What you lost here is nothing compared to what you may lose out there."

She didn't look back. Her legs pushed her down the hall, and in a split moment she could see the purple wallpaper returning. She knew she was returning to the haunted house.

"Rachel!" she heard up ahead. The lioness squinted her eyes, but soon saw Allen running towards her. "Rach—" Before he could finish, Linus appeared from behind and grabbed the wolf.

"We're not done playing yet, Allen." A raspy laugh flowed into the wolf's ears as Linus snapped his fingers. In that instant, the pair were gone. Rachel was met with an empty hallway, just her and the damp, dingy carpet beneath her. As she looked up at the ceiling, she could see more cracks appearing around her. The wallpaper started to fall, dancing softly as it touched the floor.

"Allen!" she screamed, wanting to find a way to stop what was happening, but he was too far gone. Panic started to settle in; images of Linus torturing her friend started to flash in her mind. Linus biting through Allen's shoulder; Linus tearing his arm off his body; Linus fisting Allen with his claws ruining the wolf's insides. She hated every bit of anxiety that was flowing through her body. "Fuck!" she screamed, trying to find a way out, but there was nothing. Just her and the hallway. Her and the house she wished she'd left hours ago. Tears started to fall down. Any hope for her friends vanished from her and in that moment, she felt adrift at sea; nothing but her and her loneliness to keep her company.

"I'm afraid you can't leave yet, darling. I have one more thing to show you," Linus screamed as he returned from whatever room he came from. The goat ran swiftly. As she tried to get out of the way, he caught her, shoved his hands over her eyes and said, "Just wait. You'll understand it all, soon enough."

LOVE IN THE TIME OF DEATH

"So, you come here often?" He flashed his wallet to the server while his spotted fingers circled the rim of his cocktail.

"Thank you, officer. I'll wipe your tab for the night," the server said as he walked away. A fuckin' cop that gets free drinks at a bar. Not a bad pick on a night like that night. My eyes trailed over his body, taking him in. His hair glowed crimson underneath the bar lights, his white and black spotted fur soaking in the low blue neon from our table. The dalmatian was a hot choice, and it had been too long since I'd had a hot piece of meat like him.

I wasn't used to seeing them in plain clothes. Most of the ones on hook up apps liked to show off their uniform, as if their power trip knew no bounds. But that was who they were, fuckin' cockroaches.

"It's not my usual, but I needed a change," I responded distantly, eyes trailing to the others in the room with us. Most were scattered about; even after the virus had hit, we still craved social interactions. A slow synthwave played in the background as we shared a table. TVs on the walls showed news reports of the latest deaths. We were living in an unprecedented time, but it didn't matter. We were creatures of habit. Creatures unable to remain without physical interactions. Internet calls and social media only took us so far when we craved seeing the sky at night outside of a bar. I guessed I was no different. I took a sip of my drink. I rarely had alcohol, so I made it last. Besides, I couldn't get drunk that night. I had my mission and he was sitting right before me. My red fur glowed. We were a colorful pair, though when the lights went out, he would be devoid of anything except the blood red hair buzzed on his head. "What brings you out on a night like this? Aren't you afraid of getting sick?"

He kicked back in his seat and laughed wildly. "No illness can take me." A confident one at that. I loved it when those bastards were cocky. He knew he was gonna get his baton worked on and now he was flexin' to me. As if I'd be so impressed. Fuckin' cops. He guzzled the last of his drink and waved at the bartender for another. I smiled, thinking of getting him alone tonight, admiring his cut torso. I liked them confident, and he was brimming with it.

"I've never met someone so full of themselves," I said teasingly, taking my hand and stroking his forearm. His face contorted for a moment, then eased as I touched him.

"I've never met a stoat so talkative." It was cute that he tried teasing back. I indulged him and chuckled briefly, although a part of me hoped my remark hurt his ego just a touch. I didn't want to lose him, but I could have a bit of fun while I waited.

"I could talk your ear off all night, puppy. Just have to follow me home," I said with a wink. The boy smiled and nodded towards the door. "It's a short walk," I said as we got up and left. He stumbled for a moment and I carried him against my shoulder. The pup was drunker than I thought. That night would be easy. "Let me carry you, puppy." I dragged my tongue along his cheek, then nibbled his ear. The boy let out a small moan as we walked outside. My hand lingered down his back, grabbing his ass firmly as we ventured around the block. The neighborhood was quiet most nights, and tonight wasn't an exception. Barely anyone wanted to be out at night; most of the neighbors were old. A night of partying was never something they would indulge in, at least not anymore.

"How much farther?" the words oozed through his teeth, a small slur from the alcohol in his system. His breath was bad. Every second he opened his mouth was like a keg pouring out last month's ale. The stale air of alcohol he breathed out each time was obnoxious, but I could handle it for a few moments. I just had to get him into my door.

"Not much, baby. I'm just two more houses down." He was heavy. I didn't mind carrying him, but damn, was this drunk bastard a pain to hold.

I could hear their growling in the distance. The world was theirs at night, whatever those feral, frothing beasts were. Some said zombies, others said demons sent by God, but no god would create an existence as bleak as theirs. We'd learned to live with them; at least that was what our leaders pushed for. But that was all politics.

In the distance, a trashcan tumbled over and I saw it. A figure standing, staring at us. It was a mere shadow under the moonlight, but I knew what it was. The driveway to my home wasn't much farther. I pulled my prey along with me, his body getting drowsy as he leaned against me. "Let's go," I said sternly, yet low enough for the beast not to hear. As we neared my home, I saw it running for me. I grabbed the dalmatian and dragged him up to my porch. Trying to find my keys, I saw it getting closer. I cursed myself for not planning for simple problems like that, then grabbed a plant from my porch and chucked it at the creature coming for us. It tripped the moment it was hit, scrambling on the ground as I found my key and pushed us both inside.

I pushed the dalmatian into my home. He tripped onto the floor, which was expected considering how much he drank. "What was that?" he asked as he tried to pick himself back up.

"It's one of the infected. You've never seen one?" I responded, locking the door behind me, and baring it shut. I didn't need any intrusions tonight.

"I mean, I have on TV and stuff, but never in person." He just sat there, like a child shocked at learning something horrific.

"Still think you're invincible?" I asked playfully as I bent down and grabbed his crotch.

He shook it off the moment my hand made contact. He pulled me and started licking my neck. "Ain't nothin' in the world can kill me."

We didn't make it to the bedroom. I stretched him out on the couch and started to unzip his pants. It'd been awhile since I'd been with anyone, since I'd had the need to bring anyone home. I lowered his briefs and slid my tongue along his sheath. I always liked them musky, and the moment I latched onto his cock, I was hit with his stench. I could feel my cock get hard as I huffed him. I slid along his balls, waiting for his cock to peer out. He let out a brief moan, his cock poking out the moment my tongue touched him. I moved my mouth along his body, his abs, his neck. I kissed him hard, as it had been years since anyone kissed me; as I hadn't felt the warmth of another body and needed it. I could taste the cocktails on his tongue. I loathed it for a second, powering through as I slid my tongue around his muzzle. He kept breathing intoxication into my mouth, and for a slight minute, I thought I might get drunk off it. It might have made the breath more bearable. The moment I felt his cock get hard, I went down and lubed it up, sucking it off 'til it became slick. Without making the boy wait, I pushed him in. I pushed myself down to his knot. Though I wanted it in me, I wasn't sure I could take it. As a stoat, my ass was not as stretchy as we made it seem. I rode him hard. The couch shook beneath us, but I didn't care. I wanted to wreck every inch of that dick.

I started to stroke myself. I could feel my climax coming quick, and I didn't care if I coated him. A swift release was any release in those uncertain times. His moans quaked in my ears. They were little quivers of anticipation, waiting for that final bit of release. Waiting for the small death to linger in our bodies.

But there was no death that was small. Even in orgasm.

I could feel his cock swell inside me. My ass rode it faster, harder. I wanted to milk every drop of cum he had in him. His hands grabbed my hips, firmly holding me down. I could feel his own hips ramming into me, pumping his orgasm into my tight ass and filing me.

Soon after I shot my load onto his belly. My cum was sent flying across his body, hitting his chest and face. Before he pulled out, he made one last pump into me to ensure the last drop was shot, then let me go.

"Fuck," he forced out.

"I take it you enjoyed yourself, pup?" I said teasingly. His whole body relaxed against me as he nodded. "Good. It's a shame I have to kill you," I said as I grabbed the lamp behind him and slammed it over his head. Glass went everywhere, but it knocked him out.

I went into the kitchen to brew some coffee. It was going to be a long night.

The pandemic started like they did in the movies. Like it had years ago when we were forced to stay in our homes. It starts with one and then it spreads. It oozes quickly from person to person touching whoever is in its path. There's never much news coverage at the start. Your leadership tells you not to worry. It's all hell. It's all hell crawling in our streets. And the moment it becomes big enough to matter, it's too late.

Gerald and I first heard about it when our neighbor Erik fell ill. We heard him one night, growling, screaming. His wife Zelda screamed when she found him. I remember the moon was bright that night. Upon first glance it looked as if it were closer to the earth than normal. Maybe that was its trick, or maybe it was getting close. It's tough to say.

We all walked out of our homes as the screams got louder. I remember hearing police sirens in the distance, but they were too late. Chaos had erupted in their home, glass breaking, thunderous crashing; every bit of war was hidden behind their home.

I couldn't pinpoint it, but when I saw the infected bearded dragon jumping across a room from the window, I didn't see any life in him. He moved, but his eyes were dead in that quick moment. Then Zelda appeared. "Stop it. Stop it!" I heard her cry. Her slender feline body stood stiff; though it was dark outside, you could see their fur stand tall in the shadows. The ocean blue cat was an aquarium of fear as we all stood waiting for the moment of their death. We all could tell what was going to happen, and although we watched, none of us went to save them. At least not at first.

The sirens were still so far away. Like a silent knife cutting through my chest, I heard the words come out of Gerald's mouth. "I'm going in, Tim," my orange rodent said while hugging me. I could feel his fur standing on edge, too, as if he questioned his decision, but he was all in the moment the words came out of his mouth.

"Don't get yourself killed," I responded, staring him down, his plump body. His fur showed bright in the darkness. As if this neon Cheeto arrived to save the day, only what danger lay ahead we didn't know. I felt my arms cross, holding myself, afraid of what was going to happen. My fingers played with the crimson of my fur.

"What's going on, stoat? What's your idiot boyfriend doing?" I turned briefly and glared.

"Fuck off, Cordelia. At least someone is doing something. The police are far off, and Zelda is going to die if we don't do anything," I spat out as quickly as I could. I was a barrage of words spewing anything that came out. I didn't have time to think. My husband was in there, and here I was waiting for him to return. As if I were waiting for a war to be over, as if I had been waiting for years. It's fucked how time is relevant that way. Some days it was years, others it was moments. Fuck time.

I watched him enter the home, kicking through the door as if he were the next action hero. When the door closed, I wondered if he would return or if he would die in that house. My eyes diverted back to Zelda, who had run away from the window. I heard her scream. I had never heard anything like that before. It came out strong, but the moment we saw the bearded dragon jump onto something, the scream faded as if getting further away from us. I saw this green creature slashing, ripping, elbows flailing wildly. I started to make my way to their window; I wanted to see if Zelda was gone, if she had left this world and was lying dead on the floor. Before I could make it, something was thrown. It took me a moment to see it, but when I realized what lay before me, dread crawled up my body.

Zelda's hand landed stiffly on grass, a little drop of blue amongst a sea of green. I always thought of her body like an ocean, her blue fur shining bright underneath the sun. And the moment I saw her hand lying before me, I realized it was like seeing a small puddle of water with blood oozing from its edges. Nobody ever told you how quickly the color faded from your body when you passed.

"Gerald!" I shouted, hoping he'd hear me, but I was too late. I saw him burst into the room and when he saw Zelda's body on the floor, he almost vomited. Taking little time, he jumped onto Erik and started to pull him away from the body, but the green beast struggled. I saw the orange rodent punch the beast in the side, hoping to subdue him, but it only made the dragon fight more. In that same instance, Erik bit hard into Gerald's arm.

Screaming, the rodent pushed Erik away, and tried escaping through the door. The police were arriving; I could see their sirens light up our neighborhood like red and blue flames enveloping us all. Gerald ran from the front door, hands in the air. The police were nervous; I heard one gunshot and he was on the ground. I saw blood spew from his shoulder as the bullet grazed him. My love fell to his knees, hands still raised.

"Get the fuck down!" an officer yelled. "You fuckin' filthy rat!" I saw one man run up to my husband, gun pointed directly at his head. I knew if he were to shoot, Gerald would be dead; I knew that cop was out for blood. I imagined the life leaving his body as the officer zoomed in. I imagined a rough wind blowing through all of us; I imagined his body falling to the floor. And I imagined our home. Empty.

Before the officer could reach him, the beast appeared, grunting and groaning wildly. Drool slung from his mouth with every movement. He was very feral; I'd never known him to be that violent. It was almost like he wasn't in the body before us. As if this body was possessed and whatever piece of Erik might be in there was gone. No, that was not the bearded dragon our neighborhood knew. It was an angry shell. A shell that had burst and was creating carnage for us.

He ran from his porch and jumped onto Gerald. I watched the monster take a large bite into the rodent's neck. His screams pierced my gut and I tried to run to save him, but our neighbors held me back. I was fighting a mosh pit, fighting a sea of arms trying to reach the one person that mattered more to me and they were all keeping me from him.

That's when the police fired again, this time killing the beast that was attacking my partner. More sirens rang in the distance. An ambulance finally appeared. We watched as men in uniforms burst through the house, while others led Gerald to the first available medic. I started pushing through the crowd. I couldn't stay away from him any longer. I needed to be with him, needed to be by his side. I remember tears running down as I saw how bad the bite was, and as I approached, I heard him saying, "I don't need a hospital. Stitch me up. Just stitch me up and I'll sleep it off."

"Gerald!" I yelled as I ran to his side. "Fuck, why did you do that?"

"Someone needed to help her. I may have been too late, but someone still needed to step in." He was breathing heavy. I could see exhaustion flowing through his body. The hue of Gerald's fur faded; it was no longer the bright orange you could see in the dark. He was merely an example of what it once was. I didn't know what would happen when we went home, but I feared for our future.

"What the fuck!" Well, that didn't take long. The garage was at least somewhat soundproof, so any light screaming would be muffled. I didn't worry too much. Any loud screams would be ignored. No one there wanted to help someone attacked by an infected. "Yo, what is going on? I thought I was gonna fuck, not get murdered."

He lay on a metal table, arms and legs strapped firmly to the surface. He wasn't going anywhere any time soon.

"Murder is a rather mild way of putting it. You're a cop. You should at least know that," I said, pulling a set of latex gloves over my red fur. I always hated how it pulled, yet loved how they look. Some had to suffer for a good image. I ran my hands along the dalmatian's leg.

"Where the fuck are my clothes?" I loved how he trembled beneath my touch. There was nothing that got me harder than the smell of fear pouring from a cop's body. It was a sweet smell, a smell of musk and his shitty cologne. His breath was rushing; the alcohol was still pouring into my nostrils as he lay there. I brushed my hand up to his knee, then grabbed it firmly.

"In the trash." I stepped away for a moment, grabbing a powered hand saw, then returned swiftly, positioning it right above the dalmatian's right knee cap.

"What the fuck are you doing!" He was struggling now; his body thrashed against the table as I turned on the saw. His screams were wild then, as he did everything to get away, but there was nowhere to go. Not then, not ever. Not for him. I took my saw and smashed him in the face with the handle, then went back to his knee.

"Don't fuckin' move," I shouted, digging the blade into his flesh and turning it on. Blood splattered immediately as I tore through his fur and flesh down to his bone. Though the bones were the toughest part, the saw would still cut through. It always took a little more elbow grease than I liked.

I couldn't imagine the pain that was surging through his body, but I did sympathize slightly. I mean, if I were being sliced apart, I'd be screaming and crying like a bitch, too! I continued to saw through the dalmatian, even with the bone providing heavy resistance. It slowed down considerably, but all good things came with hard work. His screams were rapturous, slamming hard against the walls. His body started to thrash about again, shaking the table. Though he was bound tight, I worried the straps would loosen, so I took the saw's handle and smashed him in the face with it again. I pushed his head down, grabbed one final strap and wrapped it across his forehead. I said nothing to the man in my home. I started the saw and went back to work, inching my way through the bone. I could feel the end of it coming close; it just needed a few lovingly helpful pushes.

With a crack and a push, the saw went through. The leg, although tough, severed beautifully; I sat back and stared at the work before me. I pulled a cigarette off my work bench and lit it up. The moment the nicotine hit me, I was in heaven. It was that wave of sinful numbness I needed to push further. I looked down at the blood on my body, on my hands, on the saw. It was a sight I was accustomed to lately.

His sobs filled the garage. I let my eyes wander over to the dalmatian I'd brought home. I pitied him, but a part of me loved what I was doing. If I ever came to a point where I needed to stop, I wasn't sure if I could. Although it was fucked, I'd finally reached that point of deviancy that was hard to pull out of myself.

"W-why are you d-d-d-doing this?" I heard him burst out.

I didn't know what to tell him at first. I didn't know if I was ready to tell anyone that I loved doing what I do, or that it hadn't started out like this. Where does one begin? Murder was such a complicated matter, anyways. It wasn't a linear crime. There was always intent behind it. For some, self-defense, survival. For others, anger. And for the little percentage out there, fun.

I sighed, breath heavy with smoke as I pushed it out from my body. "Because I loved him. Still love him."

When we made it home from the incident, my first thought was to send the rodent to bed. I was a tad angry with him for not going to the hospital in the first place; the least Gerald could do was to get his ass in bed and sleep through the pain. My heart was heavy with worry.

"I really think you should go," I spoke out, though I knew

he'd resist.

"I'm fine. I just had a bite. People bite each other all the time!" he responded, hands spread out as if to say "what's the big fuckin' deal?"

"I don't think that's the logic you should use for a wound that looks legit fucked up," I was quick to retort, but still he wasn't having it.

"Listen, I'm fine. If it gets bad tomorrow, I'll go. But tonight? I just want to rest and maybe, if you'll indulge, a piece of that tail." I could never say not to his grin. The moment that smile trailed across his face, I was gone. I rolled my eyes and sighed heavily.

"You're going to be the death of me, rat," I said moving closer to him, my hands rubbing along his torso. "Let's get you up to bed."

We didn't know anything when the virus hit. I led him up our stairs and into our bedroom. I knew he'd be stiff, so I was gentle when I kissed his neck. My tongue ran across unbitten orange fur down his chest, his belly, only to return upward to his nipple. I felt his hands move to his crotch, unzipping his jeans open. He didn't say anything as I pushed him onto the bed. Before I jumped on him, I noticed some of his fur in my hands, but I thought little of it, figuring it was stress from the bite mark. I crawled on top of him, my shorts sliding to the wayside as I positioned myself. As I slid down his shaft, I started to notice the color of his fur lose more of its brightness. Still assuming it was from his incident, I continued to ride him. Slowly at first. It had been awhile since we'd fucked. Though the passion was never lost to us, life did make sex a secondary part of our relationship. When his cock entered me, I had almost forgotten how it felt. How thick he was, where he curved; it was as if I was relearning territory already traveled.

I heard him grunt, his hands sliding hard down my back,

then falling away from me. He started to feel stiff beneath me, my fingers pushing into his flesh only to be met with a stern wall.

"Don't stop," he whispered, his moans turning into struggled grunts as I rode faster, my own member flopping onto his belly each time I slid down.

"I've missed this." The words flew from my lips, my eyes closed; I savored every minute spent in that darkened abyss with him.

"So h-have—" His words trailed off in the darkness. His grunts got louder. I could feel everything stiffen beneath me. The faster I rode, the closer I got to my orgasm, the more he was undergoing some change in this darkness.

My body moved as fast as it could as my orgasm reached its peak. I moaned wildly as I felt myself shoot a load onto my lover's belly. The air was still when we finished. Though he had not orgasmed, his body felt looser than ever, as if he were a plush toy and I the puppeteer moving him. I leaned in to kiss his cheek, but the more I listened to the silence, the more I realized. He wasn't breathing anymore. I didn't know when he'd stopped, but he wasn't breathing then. I turned the lights on, dreading what I was about to find in our darkened room. It took a moment for everything to adjust, then I saw him. The orange nearly flushed, as if it was rotten fruit decaying every minute it was out of the earth. The man I knew as Gerald was dead. I couldn't process what was before me. I couldn't understand that his body was lifeless. I started shaking him, screaming his name. Tears ran down from my eyes as I slapped his face. I tried everything, anything to make that man wake up, tell me it was a joke, tell me I was crazy.

But he didn't wake up. He didn't move.

I left the room in tears. What else was I to do? I needed to start calling people. Needed to start making arrangements. I needed just to move. It was a wrenching pain that resided inside me. I sobbed, the wails of my cries overtaking our home. He was just so lifeless. So...dead. It wasn't like how you saw them in the movies. They weren't peaceful when they die. They didn't always look that way. He just lay there on the bed and all I could do was analyze how dead he looked.

I left the room and ventured into the kitchen. I started the flame on the stove and put a pot of tea on. I remember thinking it was going to be a long night. I didn't want to call anyone at that point. I just wanted to sit in silence. I just wanted to collect myself. I set my phone aside and sat down at our kitchen table, my mug already holding a tea back. I sat there under the dim light that hung above and just stared down the hallway. It had never felt so empty before. That whole house had never felt that way. But that night everything was empty.

The air was so still around me that the kettle sent a shiver through my body as it started to whistle. I rubbed my paws over my eyes and went to go pour the water. When I returned, I sat down, took a sip, then stared down the hall again.

My heart dropped when I saw him. He was standing there, frothing, eyes staring right back at me. Only the eyes didn't seem alive. They seemed dead. His breathing was guttural, each breath a raspy blast of air. I wanted to say something, anything to break the air, but I stayed silent. Though Gerald was before me, I had never seen him this mad before. I had to refrain myself from running into his arms.

We were dueling at this point. Waiting to see who would break the silence first. Who would be the first to move. I knew if I did, he would catch me. He could catch me and kill me like Zelda was killed. Whatever he had, I knew it was from the bite.

But Gerald wouldn't wait anymore. He bolted down the hall and right for me. I ran to the side, into our living room, expecting he would almost crash through the window. And he did. He hit the table and I ran down the hall. Although not my brightest idea, I bolted down the stairs to the basement, tripping midway. My ankle felt sprained, but I didn't have time. I started to crawl, tried to lift myself up, then I saw him. He stood tall at the top of the stairs, the light making him more shadow than monster in my home. He ran down them like I did, stumbling down midway. In some ways we were a lot alike, and this was one of the ways I felt fortunate about.

I jumped out of the way, finally coming to my feet as I ran further into the basement. We had a section blocked off with a cage. We liked to get kinky. And though I wished that was a time I was being locked up, I stepped into the area. I waited for him to run in with me. Waited to trap him in. The bars were sturdy. I ensured they wouldn't break under pressure as I wanted the real feel of steel in our home.

He bolted up, ankle split sideways. The rodent hobbled fast towards me, arms shoved out as in preparation to grab me. But he wasn't going to grab anything. The moment he walked past the gate, I pushed him away as his hands grabbed my arms. He bit at me, but missed each time. I pushed him again this time, forcing him to let go. He went for me again. I tried to kick him, but he jumped onto me, pinning me down. His spit spewed all over my face and body. I tried to keep my mouth closed; I didn't want any of it inside me. I struggled, punching him in the face, kneeing him in the balls, anything to get him the fuck off of me. But he wasn't letting up. He kept biting down and missing. He went for my neck, my chest, anything he could see to get ahold of, but his teeth just weren't grabbing. I counted myself fortunate. I did a final hail Mary and sent my head up into his, causing him to fly back off of me.

I picked myself up and he started running for me again. I ran toward him, pushing him to the back of the cage. I took his head and slammed it hard into the wall, which made him disoriented. He hobbled to the side, unable to keep his balance, and I ran for the gate door. I slammed it shut and locked it. He wouldn't be getting out any time soon.

He was still sniveling on the table. I dropped the last of my cigarette on the floor and stomped it out. "Don't fuckin' move," I said as I grabbed the leg I'd just cut off and took it with me into my home. The air was still much like the night Gerald turned, but it was always still when I did that. I walked down the hall and to the basement door. Taking one deep breath, I opened the door and started to descend the stairs. It fuckin' stunk down here. God, it was horrible, but I guessed the dead still rotted. Pinesol would not make that any better. I knew the leg was dripping with blood, but decided I'd clean it up later. I wasn't going to have visitors any time soon.

I could hear him growling. It pained me each time to hear the guttural noises emitting from his mouth. The moment I reached the bottom stairs, I turned on the lights. I always hated how they put the switch at the bottom. Some people liked to see as they go down, but I guess the developer was like "nope, you gotta learn the hard way, fucker."

Gerald was looking worse. Bits of his flesh and fur were gone. They rotted away like nobody's business. I wanted to try and embalm him, but I didn't want to kill him, nor would he let me get close enough to do it. The other day, his cock fell to the floor and I reached in and grabbed it fast. It was in the cooler as I worked out how to make use of it.

His intestines were hanging out of his belly. He'd ripped it open one day running against the bars. They trailed to the floor like tentacles. Only I couldn't get fucked by them. He was a mess of a rat. At least I didn't have to worry about clothes. The bastard didn't have any on. God, he fuckin' smelled. Some days I wondered how I could love something like that, but he was good once. He was decent. Maybe he'd come back one day. Some days I believed this would all go away and he'd return as if we were together. Wishful thinkin', right? I supposed it also helped that I'd enjoyed the taste of murder, too.

He was aggressive the moment I tried to open the door. I pushed it back hard and hit him, then threw the leg at him. He didn't miss a beat. I heard his teeth gnawing into the bone. I didn't want to watch him eat it, but I could hear the blood splatter as he ripped a bit of flesh out.

I ascended the stairs. Although I still loved him, the line between love and the joy of killing were blurring for me. The moment I went back up there, I was going to chop up the dalmatian on my table. God, he'd been a good fuck. I should probably take his cock and put it with Gerald's. At least I'd get some "me" time out of it.

The moment I started sawing into the dalmatian, I knew I was going to love it. I was gonna love hearing him scream, hearing him beg, hearing him offer me everything under the sun. But the sun had given me that, the taste of blood, and boy did I love it. My first kill was exhilarating, to say the least.

The Niblock's boy up the street had just turned nineteen. Though the police banded together to find him, they never found his body. Nor his phone, nor any trace of him. It was interesting how cops all banded together, even when their kids were involved, yet they still didn't have a problem with murdering the rest of civilians. Well, the little cat didn't know what he was getting into when he messaged me on Murr. But it didn't matter, I still had some fun with him before feeding the boy to Gerald.

Then there was the cop who put the bullet in my Gerald's body. The one who almost killed him, who would have killed him if he hadn't been stopped. God, I hated them fuckers. One of the few times I topped a bitch was 'cause I didn't want that German shepherd cock inside me. Fuck the police. I fed him to Gerald so quick. His cop buddies still didn't know.

How time flew. I walked back to the garage to find the lights off. Immediately, I knew he was gone. I knew the bindings were wearing quickly. Just what I got for buying fake leather. I walked into the darkness, turning the lights on when I found the switch. As I suspected, he was gone. I moved further in, looking around. I started to follow the trail of blood he left behind. *Stupid dog*, I thought. His leg was gone; he couldn't move far. Smirking, I started to sing, "Where, oh where has my little dog gone? Oh where, oh where could he be?" until I stopped in front of a large freezer. The trail ended there. It was large enough to hold a body. Large enough to hide in. I was certain he was in there. I put my hands on the lid and pulled it open. But nothing was there. "What the fu—" I was tackled before I could finish. Where he was hiding, I wasn't sure, but this bitch was going to get a slow death. I knew that.

He pinned me to the ground and screamed into my face. "Oh puppy, you shouldn't be up. You're already losing a lot of blood," I said, looking at the trail on the floor. I went up and bit him hard in the face, ripping a chunk of his cheek. I spit it back at him. He couldn't hold me after that; his hands went for his face and I headbutted him off of me. I grabbed my meat cleaver from the workbench and slammed it hard into his head. I rammed it again, and again, blood spewing everywhere. His face was splitting apart with each swing. I could almost see his brain as I continued to chop him open. "Fucking bitch," I grunted out, only then realizing he was dead.

I sat back, breathing heavily after exerting myself. It was

like I had just orgasmed a fourth time that night. I let my breath catch up. Let it calm my body, then lifted the bitch onto the table. I pulled out a clipboard of names. All his little partners. I crossed Officer Jones' name off my list and set it aside. I wondered for a moment who I would find next, but pushed the thought away. There was a time to make plans, but not that night. I brushed my hand along his body, preparing to carve the rest of him up. I didn't need to strap him in. I just needed to get started. Gerald wouldn't be hungry again soon.

DOWN INTO THE INFERNO

I had never been inside the club before, but he was missing. I'd seen it from the outside. Seen pictures of him standing under the bright neon lights just before he ventured through its doors. I always loved how the lights would turn Cliff's antlers blue, or his fur a darker shade of brown. Cliff was all about that life, all about seeing the night through 'til dawn. I could still see him if I closed my eyes, harness tight around his chubby body, bright pink jockstrap, and a cigarette in his mouth. When he had that on, I knew he was going to the club. I knew where he'd be. I knew he'd be home. Until he didn't come home.

That night, I was going to get answers. No shit from nobody. I stood tall in front of the club, ripped denim jacket clinging tight to my purple fur. I loved how it glowed underneath the neon lights. I didn't pretend to be skinny. What bear normally is, right? My pants clung to me and I wore my harness proud. I had never been to a club like that. I had never been to any club outside of a punk show. I slid my paw around the top of my spiked hair, green spires standing tall from my skull. My pants clung tight to my body and my belly hung out for a bit, but it didn't matter.

At Nasty Jack's they called me the cannonball of fury as I rolled through the skinny boys at the hardcore shows. Well, it was time to put my skills to use.

I strolled up to the club entrance. There wasn't anyone outside, and the door was locked, so I just knocked. My fist was large enough to shake the thing off its hinges, then I saw a set of eyes peering through. "Open up," I said, my voice still raspy from screaming at the Tailhole Surfers a week back.

"Aren't we bossy today?" The eyes rolled and I heard the locks click and the door open.

"Yea, yea. Just open the fuckin' door before I kick your ass." Sometimes my mouth was bigger than my dick. This giant-ass rhino stepped forward and ushered me inside.

"I don't think you got the balls, rodent." I wasn't going to correct him. I just pushed through eyeing him up and down to stay tough. I knew one punch from him would practically kill me. "Word of advice. Leave all your expectations here, punk. What's around that corner ain't like what you seen." I didn't say anything in return. I just nodded and pushed my sunglasses up a notch.

I didn't think it was going to be bad. I'd heard stories, seen some pictures, but how much of it was true? I imagined if a club was that bad, it'd have been shut down by then. I moved onward. I had my mission. I knew what I was there to do. I moved into the club area and the moment I walked in there was just a sea of bodies. Clothing was a choice, and most decided against it. From afar I could see the strippers and thought I'd start there. I felt like the 80's rubbed its dick all over my face the more I stood in the place. Not that it was a bad thing, dick or the 80's, but, y'know. It was a thing.

I started to make my way through the dance floor. It wasn't unlike what I was used to, only more coordinated and your purpose wasn't to murder the guy you were bumping into. An owl pushed his wings outward, his glitter jockstrap almost blinding me from the neon hitting his crotch. I laughed; Neon Crotch would make for a good band name.

I took a seat at the first dancer I found. The rabbit kept his ears down. I watched his neon blue body slide down a golden pole, then looked at his cock cage. It didn't look like you could unlock it. I could never wear a cage like that. At some point I'd need some release, otherwise I'd go mad and murder everyone. But that could also be the anger talkin'. I stopped analyzing it a long time ago. I nodded at the dancer and slipped a few bills in front of him. It wasn't long before his twink body hopped onto my lap. "You don't look like one of the regulars," he said loudly. The synth-wave beats seemed to go on forever, but everyone loved it there.

"I'm looking for someone. Maybe you know him," I said. I showed him a picture on my phone and he turned quickly.

"I might." His ass slid along my belly. I could feel my cock rage against my pants. I'd never had a dance so personal. His hands wrapped around my head, fingers running over my spiked hair. The dancer moved in and started to slide his tongue along my cheek. "You could always have more...for an added tip." There was always a price. The rabbit slid his hips hard against my crotch, a hand trailing down my chest. "I'm the best there is in this place. Won't get a better ride than me." He was really selling hard. My cock raged against the tightness of my pants. I wanted to slam him on the dance floor and wreck his hole. I started to slide my hands along his blue fur, my claws teasing his ass as I slid down. His mouth slid along my neck, and as I was about to throw a chunk of cash down at him, I felt something off. His teeth were sharper than any rabbit I had ever encountered. As if his mouth was made of porcelain, hard enough to penetrate beneath my flesh, strong enough to do damage to my throat.

I pushed him back, pushing my mind back to my mission.

Though his tight twink body was tempting, his teeth gave me a weird vibe. His eyes glowed through the neon lights flashing around us. I could hear people behind me fucking on the floor. Giggles, moans, gasps; it was a war of sex coming from all sides of us. "What happened to him?" I asked plainly. I knew something had happened. I knew he was either dead or coked out of his mind.

I could see the disappointment in his eyes. He was eager for a fuck. Eager to join the orgy that surrounded us. But there was plenty of dicks around. A tight ass like his wouldn't take long to find a willing trick. "You'd have to talk more with Ricky. He's the skinny gold rat in the corner." He nodded his head towards the bathrooms. I saw who he was talkin' about; looked like a twig tweaker waiting for another round of meth. "All I know is your boy never left the club." The dancer was getting up quickly. "Dance is over, babe, unless you got another few bucks to give me."

"If he never left, where in this place could he be?" I asked him, tossing another couple bills on at him. How did one not leave a club? It wasn't that big and it didn't look like anything was going down there. It was like a normal dance party.

"You'll see. There's several levels here." The boy blew me a kiss and returned to his pole. For a brief moment, as I watched a wave of blue glide down the golden pillar, I thought of calling him back. I was horny then; my body felt pent up, urging to release every ounce of cum into this hot fuck. But I decided to move onward.

I felt raindrops fall on my head, and it took me a moment. I stared upward to find out what the fuck dribbled all over my fuckin' hair only to see platforms hanging from the ceiling. I saw two shadows up there, and then I realized. They was fuckin! Them motherfuckers jizzed all over my fuckin' face, didn't they? A neon strobe light hit them and I saw one person on the platform suspended by their arms, hooks stabbed right through their arms. There was a pig up there, his dick deep into the person he hung. The platforms above held couples, one a pig, the other I couldn't get a good eye on, all around, each doing something extreme. Something different. The pigs were never affected. Their partners, though— God, it was rough.

As the neon lights flashed, I was able to make out a cat on her knees. I moved my head to try and find the whole picture above, seeing a toy stuffed up her ass. Her pig top was naked, sporting a lightning bolt over this bulging belly. Her arms were bound to the railings of the platform above, then I realized: she was being tazed. I watched her writhing as he pressed this metallic rod against her breasts. Smoke rose from her body the longer he left it on her. Her hairs stood at the edge of her flesh, waiting to jump off as waves of electricity were sent through her breasts. The pig was slow with his movements, sliding the pole down her body. I wondered how hard she was fighting the gag that kept her mouth full, her eyes wide enough to pop from her skull. It didn't take long for her top to shove the rod against her thighs. What did zapped flesh smell like from afar? She looked like a feast of spoiled meat, sizzling at the will of the pig. Did her body smell of decay when the rod was removed? What did her screams sound like right then? Were they an unforgiving wave of pain, or was she overwhelmed with the sensation of being shocked all over? I could see the marks left on her as I stood watching. Her fur remained on edge as if relaxing was no longer an option. And although I saw tears run from her eyes, I wondered how much she enjoyed it.

I wanted to be up there. I wanted to be the one shocking her. I wanted to push the top from his terrace and take his place. The thought of it made my cock rage harder than it ever has.

I was starting to see how out of the ordinary this club

was. I was used to bar fights and fucking done in private stalls. Everything about those walls screamed of a freeing pleasure I had never known until then. I was starting to love every second of that place the longer I stayed inside. What devil's dancefloor had I stumbled upon? What pandemonium of sex had I entered? And why did I not know of that before? I decided to stop watching and get moving. I made my way through the crowd again, heading towards the bathroom. Before I even talked to my target, I punched the door in. There was a party happening in one of the stalls; I could hear their moaning beneath the synth music. Lucky assholes.

I'd seen a bathroom like that before. All tattooed up on the walls, as if its history needed to be scrawled over every inch of it. It wasn't as dingy as I was used to. The owner kept it clean, as if to maintain some semblance of grime, yet provide a pristine area for the sexually adventurous. The floors were damn near spotless, lights shining perfectly off the porcelain tile as I journeyed to find a urinal. Though the music was loud outside, I could still hear my footsteps as I meandered around, eyes examining the small space I've entered. My ears flickered, picking up on a set of chains rattling slightly. Quick breaths were attacking the air as I searched for the source. I placed a hand over my chest, feeling how quickly I was breathing, but it wasn't coming from me. There was something there with me. Something afraid. Then I saw it, a large beastly painting at the last stall. They really did a number on the dragon's eyes, making it seem like the beast was staring right through your body. As if he saw everything inside you; as if he knew you before you ever met up. The red scales were fiery, like his body was made of flames and his black hair darker than any abyss I'd ever seen. The artist made him hold a set of chains and I followed them until the painting ended and the real chains emerged from the canvas.

Then I saw their bodies. A trio of wolves were bound

to the walls, their collars drilled into the drywall of the bathroom. At the start, a larger wolf, blood staining his blue arms and white belly, squirmed as his ears flickered. The wolf's eyes tried to open, but wouldn't, as if they were glued shut. I watched his jaw struggle, his lips staying shut as he worked effortlessly to pull them apart. I knew he was listening to me, listening to my steps, the rustling of my clothes. My eyes traced the roundness of his belly until settling on his package entangled in barbed wire. A large breath entered my lungs, laced with anxiety.

I moved to the wolf next to him, yellow fur chained to those bathroom walls. I studied his arms, where the bones were broken, sticking out from his flesh. A sharp pain shot through my elbows the moment I saw his hanging by the thread of his fur. He didn't squirm, as if moving would rip his flesh open and although he'd be free, he would be without his arms. My eyes trailed down the muscled beast, his eyes stapled shut. Though small, I could see the thin pieces shining under the light. His head jerked, moans leaving his throat but held back from his shut mouth. The longer I studied, the more I saw the twine holding it shut. My belly rumbled in the silence between us. I could feel the fear roaming all throughout my body as I took my eyes off of him.

The third one wasn't even alive. I stared at green fur going pale as I saw a body with his throat slashed open. Chains were wrapped around this wolf's forehead, holding him against the painting as if the other two weren't enough of a warning. This slender twink of a wolf decayed with two living victims who would soon meet the same fate. On his chest I read the words etched in the white of his fur, "Can you see?" My eyes bolted back up to the picture and I saw the words, written in a crimson red. As if it were their own blood. "Don't fuck the dragon."

It seemed that club was not without its secrets. My heart

started to race, realizing my Cliff was still there, realizing he could be suffering a similar fate as those three warning pieces before me. Shaking slightly, I stepped back and strolled up to a urinal. "Oh, what the fuck?" I said as I looked down, only to see it was a person. I stepped back to see an assortment of bodies all chained to the bathroom wall. I'd say they were blindfolded, but it seemed much more malignant than that. Their blindfolds were drilled into their heads, hands drilled against the walls, and chains bolted around their neck. I really had to piss, and though the dark nature of this place was starting to become polarizing, I was not below a touch of piss play. I chose the first fox I saw. His mouth was forced wide open by some form of gag. I'd seen them before; pretty much every dentist used them. I looked to the stalls and wondered if the same was in there, or worse. I knelt down and smoothed my hand over the fur of the orange and white fox before me. His belly trembled as I touched him. Holy fuck. They were all alive.

I couldn't not use the boy in front of me, so I took a piss in his mouth. The boy let out a few soft moans, but didn't try to struggle. I wondered how long he had been there. How long he had been bolted like this. Then I wondered if he wanted it that way. I'd seen it before; some folks just desired to be an object. I didn't always get the psychology behind it, but it was there.

I found a stall where moans were coming from and knocked. "Say, any of you think you could help me find someone?"

"Fuck off!" someone said from the inside. Pretty rude thing to say, but I guessed that was what I got for interrupting their fuck fest. It still pissed me off.

"I hope you choke on it, fuckwad," I yelled back and started to exit the bathroom. I returned to neon Armageddon. The more I paid attention, the more the club got weird for me. At first it seemed like your normal BDSM club, but meat hooks and nailed urinals were on the more extreme side for me.

Was this what Cliff was into? A dalmatian sporting red spots crossed my path; he was leading a submissive in a suit. As I stared at it longer, I saw how the suit was sewed into the flesh of the sub. There was no leaving the suit without ripping your own skin first. The sub looked at me, its tail like that of a husky. It wagged as it saw me and ran up to jump on my belly. When I saw its eyes, I realized one was sewn shut as well. I didn't want to know if he did the same to the mouth, or worse. There was only one part of its body exposed aside from the ass, and that was a piece of its cheek. Underneath the neon, you could read the dalmatian's signature, burned directly into the body of this gimp.

I didn't have time to think about what was around me. That wasn't my style of bondage, but who was I to judge? Everybody's got their thing. I saw him at the bar. Little rodent. He and the rat bartender were having a drinking contest, it seemed, each pouring mugs of beer down their throats. The bartender pulled the mug away and slammed it down on the bar, breaking the glass upon impact.

That was more my speed. The bar was packed. Bodies were everywhere, dancing, drinking, fucking. I was starting to get used to the atmosphere. My club wasn't so different from there; just less fighting, less rage. And maybe that was what this place got right, funneling rage into another sexual use. Either way, I could see myself coming back any night.

I took a stool next to the duo. "Whiskey," I said as I looked at the orange rodent I was told to meet.

"What's a punk asshole doing in a club like this? Doesn't seem like your scene," the bartender asked.

I didn't care to ask his name. I lowered my shades and looked at them both. "I'm lookin' for someone," I said as I pulled out my phone and showed them Ray's picture in front of that club. "Any of you boys seen this guy here?"

The bartender shook his head. "Everyone's a body here. I don't pay attention much to who runs in and out."

I slammed my fist into the bar. "Listen, you fuckin' pie—"
The orange rat put his hand on my shoulder.

"I'll tell you, if you indulge me for a moment." I could see the smirk slide across his face. He placed two tablets on the grimy, flat surface and pushed one to me. "Take one, then we'll take a room." He nodded over to the bartender who. handed him a key. When my whiskey was set on the bar, I gulped it down in a swig and popped the pill.

I'd had them all before. All drugs worked mostly the same; they only produced different results. You still got high. You still had fun. The orange rat led me behind the bar. The moment the door was shut behind us, he locked it and grabbed my crotch. "The pill should be workin' in a few minutes."

"What'd you give me?" I asked him, my cock starting to get hard. He wasn't the best looking guy there. Probably wouldn't have been my first or second choice of fuck, but I didn't plan on turning him down.

"I don't even have a name for it, man. It's like poppers, only the rush is ten times more powerful. It's like—" His words drifted off in the distance. The room started to spin and I could feel my pulse racing against my skull. He knelt down and unzipped my pants as I started to slide away into the atmosphere. The room's strobe light was only partially working, the red and greens and blues dimmer, but the drug made them glow bright. Grey walls and colorful lights were all my eyes could fixate on as I felt my cock enter that boy's mouth.

My heart started to race faster. My body wanted to do nothing more than rage. I could feel myself slamming my body into my mates at Nasty Jack's as the rodent boy blew me. The itch started to get stronger. I could feel the ground beneath my feet shake, and all I wanted to do was fuck and fight.

I pulled the orange boy off my dick and pinned him to the wall. He was saying something, but I couldn't hear him, I just shoved my cock into his ass, holding him down firmly. My neck pulled my head back and I roared wildly as I started to hammer my body into this rat. He seemed fairly open. I wondered when his last fuck was, as I pulled my head forward and sank my teeth into his neck. I watched his paws start to write something. I knew it was in his blood; my teeth were sharp enough to draw and splatter. I didn't pay attention; I just wanted release. I hammered faster and faster, my claws digging into that man's chest. I knew I was ripping him open. I could feel the blood all over my hands, yet I still didn't care. I fucked him hard. Used his little body until I could feel my orgasm shoot far into him. And when my load finally escaped, I let out another loud, obnoxious roar.

"Looks like you spilled first blood tonight." A voice creeped from the darkness. I spun around quickly to see who was around, and at first I saw nothing. My eyes searched deep into the darkness of this room, and slowly a chameleon emerged. His eyes wide, when his body shifted, he glowed. His neon green scales brightened the darkness between us as he approached. "It's normally not so quick, but I guess your carnal instincts just had to rage, didn't they? Or maybe it was the pill you took; that shit always makes an animal go wild. Still, ashamed you had to kill the dealer in all this."

He slithered closer to me, his hands sliding along my chest as the chameleon sniffed my neck. My fur stood on edge. I jumped back quickly, my paws pushing the neon creature back. "Yo, what the fuck, man!" I said as my eyes sized him up. "I didn't mean to kill him. I'm just here to find somebody.

I didn't want to kill this guy. Here, look at this picture! Do you know this deer?" I was getting frantic. My words started to sputter from my lips as I kept looking back at the dead rat before us both. "He was supposed to help me!" I shouted. I didn't know what to do. I didn't know how to handle the life taken by my own hands. I'd gotten into a lot of fights, but I'd never killed anyone before. I'd never had to see the aftermath of a war lying right in front of me. His body looked mangled, as if seven cars had run through every inch of his torso, intestines spilling through his belly. "Fuck!" I shouted as I kept seeing the lifeless eyes staring back at me.

The chameleon looked over Cliff's picture, his fingers rubbing his chin as he studied the photo. "Oh, yeah. I remember him." His words were careless, as if Cliff were an afterthought. As if the body bared no importance to him, and that may have been true, but goddamn, did he mean a lot to me. I could feel my phone cracking under my grasp as I listened to that fuckwad talk. "He's been down in the dungeon. He's with the dragon, and sweety, nobody leaves the dragon's lair. Especially on a night like tonight." I didn't want to believe my eyes at first. The chameleon bent down and started to lap at the blood spilled on the floor. His body started to morph into something indescribable at first. His back crunched as it arched, forcing the body to get longer. His arms started to extend like skinny twigs being pulled from a tree's branch. For a second, I could see his spine getting sharper, as if he were growing spikes along his back. His hands started to stretch out as he cradled the dead rat from the floor. "You may want to get there quickly, though. You've spilled blood, and now we can come out. We've been hungry for so long." I had never heard a voice so deep before, as if his breath emitted hellfire. I watched this changing body devour the body, sucking in fur and intestines as if eating a spaghetti dinner. I heard each crunch as he tore bits of flesh from bone.

He flashed his eyes at me like headlights in a storm. I didn't know what was happening, but I couldn't watch much more. This glowing beast was finishing his meal and I knew I'd be next if I didn't leave. A sense of dread pounding in my chest, I ran through the door and saw them all waiting for me.

I stood before an apocalypse. Bodies were shifting everywhere before me. Claws outstretched, arms widened, I could see their fur stretching as they grew larger. They were a sea of growing bodies, each one getting bonier, sharper, blood splattering as they morphed into whatever unholy creatures they were. It rained red from the ceiling, drops slamming onto the floor as I looked above me. The pig I envied was shifting, his cat partner still bound to the railings. I tried to look into her eyes, but she was staring at her top, staring at the monster he was becoming, his snout pushing further from his face as his teeth started to fall from his mouth. I squinted to get a better look, seeing sharper teeth growing. Then I saw her face, the terror that started to form in her eyes. He grabbed her head, eyes glowing like flashlights, and dug his mouth into her neck. "Fuck!" I shouted, looking down and at the crowd before me.

They were a barrage of headlights staring at me; all the same, as if all the cars aligned, preparing themselves for an inconceivable carnage. And there I was, the prey waiting for the inevitable end that was coming for me. The music swayed in the background, slow, like a suspended bridge in a storm, ready to break into the chaos kept hidden behind their eyes. They stood around, a corpse lying on the ground. The dead body of an orange maned wolf glowed in the center, the club lights singling her lithe body out in front of the sinister group surrounding us. A tigress knelt over this woman's body, forcing her chest open. Her breasts parted as blood spewed upward into the air. I could hear the ribs cracking as this demonic tiger shoved her hands in the corpse's chest, yanking its heart out, and tearing into it with her teeth.

I couldn't blink without someone new appearing on this corpse. From the floor, a brown stoat slithered through, bones sticking out sharp along this creature's back as he latched his teeth onto the body's leg. "Don't need this leggie now, bitch," he growled out as he ripped a chunk of the body's thigh from the bone. As he chewed on the flesh and fur, an arctic fox latched onto an arm, teeth shredding through the corpse's elbow and severing the lower arm. They feasted as if starvation was all they knew. As if every moment they lived was filled with a hunger they couldn't satiate.

Every beast before me carried the same features; elongated snouts and teeth more carnivorous than I had ever seen, some extending out of their muzzles. They all growled lowly, as if waiting for the right moment to strike. Most had lost the fur on their faces, only wearing skin pulled over their long faces. I had never seen bodies so stretched, so leathery, so wrinkled by the bones underneath them. What hell lay before me? What had I brought myself into?

And then the boy who danced on me, I saw him in the center of the crowd, and all eyes turned to him. He was no different than the other beasts there. He walked directly up to me, his ass jiggling in his jockstrap. My hands still wanted to grab his bulge; I wanted to wrap him in my bear arms and fuck him, as if he were still the dancer I met before. As he neared me, I could see bits of his blue fur ripped from his torso. I imagined the shift from person to demon did not leave you scathing hot, yet my dick still stood firm for him. "You'll have to get through all of us to get to your boy, dear bear. Are you sure...you can take it?" His hands trailed up my arms as he moved in to kiss my cheek. His tongue licked all along my neck, lips clamped tight. I felt my hands grab the boy's sides as I pulled him closer. His teeth were scratching at my flesh, and although I knew he was going to bite me, I didn't care. I let them sink into my fur and flesh as his claws grabbed at my waist. They dug into my side and I roared as the pain surged through my body. My arms pulled this lithe demon from me and I held him high underneath the neon lights. My hands around his neck and head, I roared again, as if instinct was driving me to do it.

"I'll kill all of you bastards!" I screamed as I twisted his neck like a bottle cap. Quick, easy; the way I liked it. I took his dying body and tossed it into the crowd.

My eyes searched through the crowd of glowing eyes, and that was when I saw him. The bartender kept his head down, cleaning a glass, and I shouted to him. "Yo, fuckwad! The dungeon! Where is it at?"

"If you can get through the crowd, it's straight back. One door, although if you go down there, don't expect to come back. Inferno isn't a place for people who want to live. The beast down there has been collecting, and he will add you to his mass of bodies." I didn't have time to ask him why everyone had shifted into something monstrous. I had one more tablet of rush on me. I stuffed it in my mouth and let it take over. If it made me kill the dealer, then I could at least kill a few of the demons that stood before me.

"Just a normal bar fight," I told myself as I felt the tablet kicking my adrenaline up. I let out a wild roar and rushed into the crowd, slamming my fist into anyone that stood in my way. I headbutted a few as I continued to rush through. There was no parting sea, at least not for me. Not tonight. I felt someone slash my back and I turned around and grabbed their face, slamming my thumbs into their eyes. I was all rage. All anger. All aggression. I had never felt this good before, but goddamn, did I feel it now. I picked up that person's body and tossed it before me. Some tried to catch the demon, but made a way for me to pass through anyways. It didn't take long for the bar to break out in chaos.

We were talking my style then. Everyone started fighting each other, distracted from the one non-demon in the room.

At least I thought they were demons. I didn't know, but my gut wasn't telling me much different. I raged against everybody that was around me. I felt some bite, some slash; I was taking wounds, but I couldn't be bothered by that. I knew my goal. I knew I would lose whatever in order to make it. The music played louder, the slow synthwave beats jamming softly as the bass boomed in our brawl. The closer I got to the end, the more I saw everyone was just fighting with themselves. What chaos were they meant to bring?

I finally found the door. Pictures drawn by the patrons were splattered all over, each dragon taking on a different form. Different colors. I didn't care, though. A body was thrown through the door, opening it right up, and I shuffled through.

I came to a set of stairs spiraling down, thought it only looked like a flight or two. As if descending into Inferno, I started to make my way down. Immediately, I started to feel hotter. The pill I took was starting to wear off as I made it to the last step. A large neon red light painted over everything in the hall before me. Flames were painted on the walls, although I wondered if I would get burned by touching them.

I journeyed across cracked cement and a narrow hallway; the basement resembled an abandoned building. As I neared a door, I could hear chanting, although the language was unintelligible. The heat was driven up the closer I got. It was almost unbearable, but I had to see that through. Two steel doors stood before me, handles curved to the side. The grey paint was chipping off of them. I could see the rust spreading to the top of the doors as I grabbed the handle.

The moment my hand made contact, the chanting stopped. My fur stood on edge as I was enveloped by silence, a still air that only came when hell was near. I'd only felt that air once before, and I knew it in my gut. I knew whatever was behind that door was an agony I wasn't ready to see, but like it or not, I pushed onward. I pushed through the door and covered myself in the room's crimson red lighting. I wasn't ready for what was behind it.

There were bodies nailed on all fours, fucking machines pounding rapidly into their asses. Most wore hoods, making them unidentifiable. They were all slender bodies, blood oozing from their wounds. I wasn't sure how long they had been fucked by those beastly machines, but I could see blood splattering back each time the dildo pulled out.

Above me hung cages. Hooded bodies were chained to the bars, each captive writhing at some sort of pain. I couldn't see it at first, but as the cages swung like a pendulum, I could see the spikes their feet were forced to stand on. Most weren't penetrated, but I did see a couple of unfortunate souls that caught the spikes through the soles of their feet.

There were a pair of tigers bound to St. Andrew's crosses. I watched as a pair of slender vixens drove whips into the bound bodies, their leather shining hard beneath the lights. Their breasts only slightly exposed, they wore their clothes tightly. As I studied further, I saw the edges of the whips holding hooks. Each time they threw it at the tiger's bodies, a piece of fur and skin were ripped back into the air. The room was a war of screams, a war of moans.

Then I saw the beast, sitting on his throne like a king. I was taken aback by his muscled body. His hair slid down to his shoulders, a thin, straight abyss overtaking the blood of his scales. He was drinking a glass of wine, or maybe it was blood; I couldn't tell in the lighting of that room. Everything was just an ocean of red as if to tell me that only blood remained there. All life left when it was no longer needed. His eyes were just like the monsters above, only his body remained unchanged. He was like a demon, but a demon that could control his form. The white of his belly was splattered in blood from the bodies around him. I didn't know how much he had destroyed those people, but the moment his tall body stood, I wanted to kill him. I wanted to break his fucking neck.

"Keep going, slut. I'd like to get one more load into you before you're gone." I balled my fists, angered at what I was seeing. "Can you hear them above? Seems they've arrived early tonight." His eyes then fixated on me. "And here we have a visitor. Come to join the rest of the sacrifices?" he said, throwing the glass at me but missing. Cliff turned to me, his antlers twisting in the neon darkness. I saw his scarred body, wounds covering every inch of his arms, his chest, his face. Oh, Cliff. What hell he'd suffered there, I'd never know, but I aimed to get him the fuck out of there.

The dragon didn't waste time when grabbing my boyfriend by his jaw and forcing his mouth open. His claws pulled Cliff's tongue out and he bit it hard. Cliff's screams filled the cavernous room as I watched the dragon take his tongue. I roared out of anger, my body tired from the journey down there.

"That's my boyfriend you got slobbering all over your dick. I've come to take him home," I said defiantly. Cliff clung to the dragon's body. His arms wrapped around his legs as he started to nuzzle at the beast's waste. I knew then that he wouldn't go willingly. I knew he was determined to stay, but how much hell can you put yourself through? "Cliff, come home with me. We can get out of here. You can be safe. Please!" I pleaded to my boyfriend, but he held firm. He was a part of the inferno now. But I was still willing to fight the fires of war to bring him out of the death he was seeking.

The dragon shoved my deer to the side and walked down from his throne. I had to admit he was kind of hot, but I couldn't let that distract me. I wished for a moment I had one more pill, but figured I'd have to fight that fight without. I clenched my fist, prepared to take the first shot at this dude.

"Sir Drake," I heard someone say behind me. I turned around to find a koala looking out of the doorway. Their eyes were wide as she spoke again. "They're here."

I could hear them. The demons from the bar. They had all made their way down to the dungeon, and before I could blink I was overrun. Demons on one end. Dragon behind me. This was about as hopeless as all get out. I could hear my heart pounding beneath my chest as I heard them approaching. I turned around and he was standing behind me. He drove a fist into my face and I didn't think twice. I punched him in his belly, yet it hurt me more than him. He grabbed me by the throat and lifted my body in the air. I hated how dragons had tougher flesh than most of us animals. I tried to dig my claws into his neck, but they weren't sharp enough. A smile traveled across his face as he dug his claws into my belly. A roar tried to escape, but his grasp was too tight.

I took my paws and covered his eyes, digging my thumb into one of them swiftly. I didn't know how else to get him. He screamed, but only twisted his hand that was inside me. After a moment of us toying with each other, he dropped me. I tried to crawl over to Cliff, tried to reach the body I had come to fix, to bring home and make him whole again. I reached out for his thigh, but Cliff kicked back at me. "Babe, please!" I shouted out, and he slammed his foot into my face. "Fuck!" I screamed as I tried to get to my feet. In that brief second I stood up, I watched this blue blur run into me, grunting wildly as his antlers penetrated my body. I had never heard a shrill so wild before. He was like a pig grunting at his kill. His antlers wiggled their way inside me as he tried to pull them out. The moment he pushed back, a pair of the demonic figures I'd escaped from grabbed me. Their bony structures enveloped my body, almost cutting through my arms as they squeezed me tight. I watched as the dragon took his throne, holding his eye firmly.

The demons were not with loyalty though. I watched as he fought off anything that came at him. "I prepare this meal for you, and you come after me?" he roared as he started to bludgeon anything that jumped on his body, blood spewing over every inch of his muscled body. He was a crimson beast; blood, lust and power all wrapped up in scales and muscles. I chucked inside when I saw I could barely wound the monster.

Cliff ran up to the throne and fell to his knees. The dragon rubbed a paw over his head as he watched the chaos ensue; hooded bodies were being devoured before him. He looked down at my boyfriend and smiled wide. "You're part of the feast. Like the rest of my collection, you are here to be devoured by the walls of hell. It was so fun to ruin you before this moment." His voice was booming. I had never heard a voice so loud before without a microphone. The dragon grabbed Cliff by the throat and tossed him down the steps of his throne. "Go, and be one with the bowels of hell," he shouted. I saw Cliff's slender body fall into a sea of hands. The moment he hit the floor, the beasts were tearing into him. His blue fur ripped from his body, I watched as their twig-like arms tore at the man I came to save.

I saw the life leave his eyes, and I knew the bartender was right. There was no leaving the inferno. Not for me. Not for anyone who entered here. Pain surged through my body as I looked to my legs. There were several of them gnawing on them; others worked on my body the moment I fell to the floor. The chameleon hovered over me, moved inches to my face and whispered in my ear. "I've been wanting a taste of you since we first met." He dug his teeth far into my neck; my intestines were coming out like sausages at a meat factory. I was fading fast. I knew I couldn't stay awake much longer. My eyes started to close and the green glow was the last thing I saw before falling unconscious.

EPILOGUE

Allen appeared instantly in another room of Carnage. His eyes scurried around the dimly lit room, trying to make out what was in front of him. At first he thought he'd returned to the stadium, to the ram, to the lust still waiting for him if he died. Then he started to make out parts of a kitchen. He smelt the steam coming from a pot; turning his head to the left, he saw it funneling from the top and into the air. Fire beneath it raged against the boiling water. His eyes slowly rolled through the kitchen area again, his stomach churning at the black sludge covering the dishes a few feet away from him. His ears flicked the moment he heard buzzing. Eyes darting around, he saw a pair of roaches flying together. As he stared at them, he started to realize they were mating.

"Holy fuck, gross!" he screamed out, flapping his hands as he tried to move away. The floor was wet beneath him, his feet stumbling on the damp tile before his whole body plummeted. "What the fuck!" he yelled, feeling the grease cover his naked body as he tried to pick himself up. Roaches started to cover his hands and his feet a few at a time until he could no longer see them. "Fuck, fuck, fuck!" They started crawling up his legs, a pair making it to his crotch. He jumped up and ran for the door, but the moment his paw twisted the knob it wouldn't move. "Oh, Jesus fucking Christ." Annoyed the door wouldn't open, he looked back at the roaches piling together, as if they were making a person. His eyes squinted for a moment as he saw pieces of his boyfriend peek through. Every sliver of what lay underneath the mountain of insects was another piece of his boyfriend's fur. He watched as they shaped over the basset hound's snout, a few flying off from the tip of his nose. Allen swatted away as they moved closer, his eyes moving down the figures hands. They moved outward towards him, forcing the wolf to jump back to stay out of reach. Mike's swollen belly, his eyes peering out, his brown and white fur; it left Allen in a state of confusion. As more of Mike started to appear, panic started to surge inside him. He looked down, still naked from the earlier room. He wanted to hide. He didn't want Mike to see him like that, yet the moment he tried to move behind a counter, Mike saw him.

"Allen?" The basset hound's eyes looked over every inch of the wolf's naked body. "Allen, why are you naked? What have you been doing? I don't understand." The mass of roaches scattered, scurrying back to the inside of the walls as the hound moved towards his partner. Shock overcame his face as he reached out to grab the nude wolf standing in front of him. "I've been fucking worried about you; this place is fucked and you're just out there naked and what, huh? How many guys you fucked? Fuck, I knew you'd do this to me!" His voice got louder the more he talked. Words started to sputter out like a spinning tire stuck in mud. "Fuck, how could I be so stupid as to trust you?!"

"M-mike, it's not what you think!" The wolf moved himself back, keeping whatever distance he could. His heart started to race each time his partner got an inch closer to him. Between loud earfuls from Mike, Allen listened to the racing beat of his heart, hearing it move faster the longer he stayed in the kitchen.

"Oh, that's what they all fuckin' say! You fuckin' slut!" Mike's arm swung, forcing a pile of pots and pans to scatter from the counters to the floor. Allen let out a guttural yelp as he jumped back farther, trying to avoid the impact of being hit with a frying pan.

"If you would just trust me, babe. It's not what you think; I didn't fuck anyone!" Tears streamed down Allen's face as his eyes darted around for a weapon. *I can't get out of here without hurting him*, Allen thought to himself, a moment of sadness bubbling through his belly as he stumbled upon a cast iron pan on the floor.

"Trust you? How can I trust you when you don't give me a reason to?! I look at you and all I fucking see are dicks all over your body, you fucking slut!" Mike thrust his large, round body forward, his snout creaking back and revealing his gritted teeth as he tried to grab the wolf in front of him. Without hesitation, Allen grabbed the pan and swung it hard, hammering through the basset hound's arms and colliding with his face. The wolf didn't think twice; he swung again, hitting Mike in the head a second time. Then a third, a fourth. He kept swinging; fearful screams sprinkled with anger left his body as he pummeled every ounce of energy he had into his partner.

"I'm not a fucking slut!" The words leapt from his lips, blood splattering onto his body with each new hit he dealt. He could feel himself losing speed the more he brought the pan down into Mike's face. When he felt Mike stop moving, he tossed the pan to the side and stared down at the body. His eyes looked at the broken snout he created, the bloodied face, the missing teeth; he couldn't recognize the body beneath him anymore. A flush of emotions rushed from his feet to his heart; panic, rage, mourning all swelled inside him as he jumped back. He let out a harsh cry, his hands wiping over his face. "What the fuck have I done?" he asked to the void around him, knowing he wouldn't get an answer.

The roaches started to appear again, Mike's body disintegrated into the insects, scattering as if the lights had flushed on. I wasn't long before they covered the walls in their bodies, wings flapping every other moment. Allen's ears flickered at each leg crawling; each wing flapping, the noise of their bodies was as loud as Mike's shouting. "Stop it! Stop it! Stop it!" he shouted angrily, hands covering his ears. He wanted all the noise to go away. He wanted the world around him to be silent just for a moment. But the house wouldn't let that happen. It grew louder each time he protested.

"You killed him." A whisper pushed through the chaotic crawling of the insects. "Now who will love you? You killed the only man who ever loved you." Tears started rolling down the wolf's eyes. The words cut at him, as if taking an axe to his heart. Each letter was a swing into his body.

"That's not true! That's not fucking true!" he shouted back.

"But it is, and now you're alone. You're alone and it's your fault," the clattering of the roaches whispered back.

Allen could feel himself slipping. His mind repeated the whispers to him. He lifted his fist and drove it into his face. "Stupid! Stupid! Stupid!" he screamed out. Before him dropped a knife. He stared at it briefly, his eyes glowing in the darkness inside his roach prison.

The bugs continued to whisper to him. "Your fault. Do it. Nothing left." They repeated this chaotically. A flurry of whispers pummeled Allen's ears as his trembling hand grabbed the knife. He watched as it shook in his grasp, the steel blade wavering like a pot in an earthquake. He closed his eyes, let out a loud, mournful scream and rammed the knife in his belly. His hand twisted the blade around and slid it across, his intestines spilling out the moment the blade left him. The words broke him, broke whatever stability he carried with him in Carnage. His hands took the blade and started to slice all over his body, blood spilling down his chest and arms. He knew he would be gone soon; his vision faded quickly as his body fell over. Each time he blinked, a roach passed by. Then a foot emerged from the chaos, as if it pierced the walls of his prison. It inched forward slowly, Allen's breath getting heavier as it became harder to take in. He felt a hand on his head, felt his neck lifting until he saw him.

Linus stood in front of the wolf, holding him so he would be the last thing the wolf saw before dying. "There, there, darling. That wasn't so hard, was it? You'll make a wonderful addition to our home." The words trailed off on his ears as everything went black.

Linus dropped the wolf's body. The goat quickly knelt down, pulling Allen closer to him. Baring his teeth, his jaw clenched down into the dead body's shoulder. The room echoed with the noise of flesh being ripped away from the wolf. The goat licked the blood from his lips, his mouth full of fur and flesh; his teeth broke the meat down as he stood up. As the roaches left the kitchen and back into the walls, a large gulp fell down his throat. He went back for another bite, bone crunching as he slowly devoured the wolf's lithe body. "I imagine your friend, the lioness, will taste better than you, wolf. At least the hound had some meat on him." He ate his meal ravenously, as if it had been ages since he'd tasted anything. It didn't take long for the goat to devour Allen's body as he unhinged his jaw like a snake. The lithe wolf was quickly sucked into Linus's mouth, bits of fur remaining in the air as the goat swallowed every bit of his meal.

He stood up, licked the remaining blood from his lips and adjusted his suit. It was time for one last feast.

Rachel was slow to regain consciousness. The lioness moved her head, though each swerve of her neck was resisted. Overpowered by exhaustion, she struggled to move, a small groan leaving her lips as she started to feel the pain crawl of her arm. Rachel tried to move her fingers, slowly remembering the loss of one. Though it felt like lifting a mountain, she opened her eyes, only seeing dark blurs in front of her. *Shit, I ain't felt this bad since my last hangover*, she thought to herself as she started to feel a small jolt of energy return to her tired body. An arm moved forward, but was met with resistance. Chains echoed in the room and curved her head up. "Aw, fuck!" she screamed, realizing she wasn't leaving that house. "Motherfucker!" she screamed again, frustration building in her head. She could feel the rage startle her heart, its beating gaining speed the more her vision returned to her. Her head jolted around the room, desperation settling in her bones. *I need to get the fuck out of this shithole*, she thought frantically. She wanted nothing more than to run out of this room. Run far away from Carnage. Run anywhere that would let her stay alive. But she was bound. She couldn't leave; she couldn't see an opening or a way to break the restraints weighing her down. She hated how her arms were forced to hang above her head, how the metal held firm. Bits of fur flew in the air around her as she rattled them, writhing, pulling, anything she could do to break the bindings that held her.

Her body couldn't keep up with her rage. Rachel started to feel the exhaustion crawling back over her. She could feel herself growing tired over the adrenaline that ran through her blood. Her body was letting her know it couldn't' handle it much longer, that something would have to give. She had never been pushed that far in her life; she had never had to fear for her life, but she tried to push the fear back into her belly. *These motherfucker's ain't killing me today*, she thought as she tried to pull the chains from the ceiling. She continued to fight her bindings, thinking persistence would weaken the metal that held her captive. She pushed herself harder, knowing anything less would get her killed.

She stopped the moment she heard a door creak open. Light flushed into the room and she knew who was going to emerge from the doorway. She could feel her heart rattling harder against her chest as fear started to settle in. Her ears twitched in the darkness as she picked up the sound of footsteps. She knew who would approach her. She knew in a split moment, she would be face to face with her tour guide, the goat that started the madness to begin with. "You son of a bitch! We didn't sign up for this shit!" she screamed out in the darkness, but was met with silence. "Not gonna respond? Fucking coward! A bitch can do a lot in the dark!" She spat out on the ground. She watched it hit the concrete hard, spreading like blood against a wall. "Answer me, you fucking son of a bitch!" Each time she shouted, she could feel her anger grow. She could feel her rage burning like a forest fire in her body.

"Well, it appears our tour is coming to an end, darling." His figure started to emerge before her. His hands were forced out like a weak branch ready to leave the tree. "I hope you've enjoyed yourself on our magical, yet deadly ride. It's a shame I won't get to play with you much longer, but you and your friends sure made it all...interesting, to say the least." His hand brushed under her chin as he brought her eyes to his. Rachel had to keep herself from vomiting, the sight of his smile making her stomach turn. She did her best to keep eye contact with him, but she hated staring at the oddly shaped man before her. She hated the pentagram on his head, the crimson coat, his sharpened teeth. She hated every aspect that shaped that goat before her.

I wish I could set this motherfucker on fire, she thought, but wishes didn't come true in a house made to kill. "I just want to go home!" she protested, writhing harder against her bindings. The goat smiled wide as he walked away from her, rubbing his paw along his chin.

"Oh, sweetie, I can't let that happen now. It has been ages since I've eaten anything, and I'm so very hungry. I've been the caretaker of all these horrific things for ages, but these stories cannot remain alone. The house needs fresh blood to blend with the old. New sensations. New carnage!" His voice grew distorted with each new word. She couldn't believe her ears as she watched the figure before her. Rachel's eyes widened as she started to see a change in his body. Linus's face started to bulge, his eyes inflating like balloons as his body changed. His muzzle started to grow longer, teeth protruding from his lips. Like a dog in pain, Linus growled in agony as he felt his bones shift and become elongated stems from his body. Rachel started to panic as the goat towered over her. She had never heard someone in so much pain before, nor had she ever seen something so horrific. When Linus' legs lifted his body, a roar was forced from his throat. "Your friends were mere snacks; you'll be my main course!" His voice grew deep, a harsh raspy growl embedded in his throat as he spoke. A hand shot out and he yanked her from her bindings, chains clattering around on the floor as he brought her close to his face.

Chains still attached to her arms, she swung at him, the iron slamming right into his left cheek. The goat didn't move at the beating. He chuckled briefly as he squeezed her body firmly. "I could fucking squash you, bitch!" he said as he examined the meal he was about to stuff down his throat. Linus brought her body closer, his teeth picking at her arm, toying with her hand, then crunching his teeth down to her shoulder. He slurped the chain on her wrist like a noodle before swallowing the bits of her arm he ripped off. Screams erupted from the lioness as the pain of her arm being eaten throbbed all throughout her body. Unable to form words, she writhed in his hands, hoping he would let go.

"Poor Rachel; it'll all be over soon. I'll find your sorrow. I'll find the tale you carry and make it my main attraction!" The hulking monster growled as he lifted her higher in the air. He hovered her body, dangling her like a bundle of grapes over his mouth. His tongue slithered far from his muzzle, the pointed, slimy limb nearly reaching her. He didn't wait longer. Her body swung over him like a claw holding a prize; he counted each swing. One...Two...Three...

His fingers opened and she started to plummet towards the beastly cavern of teeth below her. Rachel's voice was starting to fail her as her screams grew quieter. Her body landed on his tongue; she felt the slimy creature wrap around her as he pulled the lioness into his muzzle. "I sacrificed a part of myself!" she finally screamed. "I sacrificed a part of myself so I wouldn't become a part of this horrible place!" Tears were streaming down her face as he halted for a moment. He savored the taste of them as they landed on his tongue. Linus thought for a moment, the devious tour guide thinking of ways to make her end an enjoyable time for him. He loved scaring anyone who entered his carnival of horrors, but that was a meal he wouldn't have for another ten years. A tale he couldn't capture for a decade. It didn't sit well with him, his stomach gurgling at the thought of going without this victim. His tongue unraveled and dropped her to the floor. The chains that remained clanked violently as she tumbled away from the towering monster.

"Your sacrifice is nothing to me. What you did to escape your hall is between you and the gatekeeper. I am, however, willing to strike a deal with you, lioness." He started to return to his normal shape, a lean, tall goat, eyes as empty as headlights. "You'll be given three chances," he started, pulling a gun from inside his coat. She watched as he unloaded the revolver, then placed three bullets in it. Silver shone bright in the dim lighting as he spun it fast, then popped it back into place. "We'll each take a turn. If you lose, I'll send you to the darkest parts of this house and make you peel your flesh off your body until I tire of you. The wallpaper needs a bit of retouching, and your blood and fur would make an excellent change. If you win, you go free."

Rachel stared at the gun before her thinking of the offer. She couldn't see an escape from it, couldn't see a way out. Her body ached at the pain she'd suffered; her missing arm, gnawed by the beast before her. She nodded, grabbed the revolver and closed her eyes. Her finger wrapped around the cold trigger and started to pull it slowly.

Click. Nothing. A wave of air left her body in relief.

Linus grabbed the gun from her, put it against his head and pulled the trigger quickly. Click. Nothing again. A smile traveled across his face as he pushed the gun into her hand.

Her body stiffened. She knew if she were to pull the trigger, she would lose the game, lose her life. Her hand shook as she grabbed it from her tormenter. The dim lights beamed off the silver sporadically as she tried to keep the weapon steady. She closed her eyes, and started to count in her head, backwards from ten. She could feel it in her gut, a bullet waiting to blow through her skull as her finger wrapped around the trigger a second time. As she made it to one, she pulled it away from her head and started to fire rapidly, as if the other bullets would demolish Linus' body.

She didn't waste any time, running the moment she knew the gun was empty. She ran down the hall, hoping to catch the first set of steps, doors, or anything. Her heart raged inside her body, panic wrapping its claws around her. She needed to get out. She'd taken her shot and now she needed to see the end of the house.

Linus waited briefly in the room, allowing the pain of his wound to surge through him before transforming again. He knew she would turn the gun on him, but what good was a game when you couldn't cheat? He waited, closed his eyes and tried to listen to her footsteps. They were loud, but runners always were. He heard her flying down the hall of Escape.

Rachel saw the hall's entrance, wishing it was a way out of the hell she'd brought herself to. Mike burst through the door. "Get me out of here!" he screamed as he saw the lioness running towards him. Her eyes focused on the basset hound as he fell to the floor. Slowing down to a job, she noticed how pale his body was, and when Mike looked her in the eyes, she knew he had already been taken by the house.

"I'm so sorry, Mike," she yelled out, feeling the tears form in her eyes. Before the basset hound could reach out for her, the hall's creatures toppled over his body and started to drag him back through the door. Rachel couldn't bring herself to watch, pushing her body to move faster, past the hall's door and to another.

"Rach!" a voice called out before her. "Rach!" She started to slow down again, looking around to find the voice calling her name. In a split moment, she realized she was in the same hallway were Allen was taken away before her eyes. She blinked once and he was there, standing in front of her. She saw all the scars on Allen's body, all the scratches, and bruises, and bites, and she knew how much he'd done to himself. Her eyes ached as she saw the linings of his guts trailing out of his belly and far behind him. Covered in his blood, his insides, she wanted to reach out and squeeze her dead friend, but she refrained. Allen's body was a map of blood, all scars connecting to the heart and spreading down his torso. Tears flooded her cheeks as she stared at the ghost of her friend. "I don't have much time. I'll have to get back to my hall soon, but you need to get out of here."

"Shit, I don't know how! Not like this place is normal. This motherfucker is dead set on killing me!" She was shouting now, her voice echoing in the hallway. She knew Linus could hear; she knew he would find her.

Allen shook his head. "I mean, I know that; I'm kind of a ghost here now. Listen, the only way to get out of here is to take a piece of him. You'll have to fight him," Allen said, causing Rachel to roll her eyes.

"Have you seen this, bitch? Really, have you seen him?" she yelled back as if to say Allen was an unreasonable prick for bringing that as her only solution. There was a brief moment of silence where the wolf stared at her; his eyes wore a dull look.

She hated when he looked that way. Hated when those eyes just sat on her as if she should have guessed what the answer would be. The eyes remained unmoved as she stared back, but she knew what Allen was saying. She knew he was telling her, "Of course; we all have, so I don't know why you're complaining. I gave you an answer." Rachel rolled her eyes, a heavy sigh leaving her body as she nodded okay to the wolf. The more she studied his face, the more she started to see how disfigured Linus had made him. At first glance his jaw seemed normal, but the moment he opened his mouth, she saw it extend wide, as if a massive cock had forced it to open in such a way. His eyes were empty, much like the rest of the dead in the house. And though his fur was already grey, she noticed how absent it was on his body.

"Thank you," she said as she tried to hug him, but the wolf jumped back before her arms could embrace his cold body. Shock shot into her eyes as she stared at the wolf. A smile traveled across his face. "Allen, quit playing," she said, but the more she stared at the smile, the more she realized that it wasn't him.

Like a coat falling from the shoulders, Allen's ghostly

figure shed from Linus. The goat stepped forward and started to change again, towering over the lioness as she jumped back. She started to run, but the hallway behind her was gone. "It's only us now, darling. You thought you were smart by shooting me." He threw his fist out, knocking her into the wall. She plummeted to the floor, bits of sheetrock and dust raining down behind her. The floors creaked around them, weak boards weakening underneath the weight of the pair. Before Rachel could lift herself up, the floor caved. Two bodies fell between boards, dust, and debris, landing firmly in a living room area.

Her vision was blurry, still trying to make out the room around her. Rachel's head pounded as she forced her aching body to lift up from the ground. Her hands slided along her sides, feeling the series of splinters left all over her from the wood. "Fuck!" she screamed out, her eyes slowly focusing again.

She didn't get a chance to look at her surroundings. A low guttural growl surged through the dust. Quickly, she took a board from the debris and started to look around. "You'll never escape." The raspy words oozed out of Linus' mouth as his body emerged from the fall. "Your home is with the rest of us, darling!" Guttural laughs filled the air as he lunged at her. His arms outstretched, he flew through the air to devour her body.

"Fuck you!" Rachel screamed, using the strength of her remaining arm and driving the wood into Linus' heart. His body fell to the floor; the lioness grabbed another board and prepared for another attack. Her eyes studied him, as if capturing prey. And although hope left her, she smirked when she saw it. Her eyes focused on his horns, seeing a crack at the tip. *All I need is a piece!* she thought as she ran forward, her hoarse screams combatting the growls of the demon goat.

Linus struggled to lift himself from the ground, his body

getting weaker from his wounds. "Stupid bitch!" he spat out as he tried to stand up. The moment he got to his knees, Rachel slammed the board in his face. Using the rest of her strength, she rammed her weapon right at the crack of his horn. "Fuck!" he screamed as a chunk flew from his body. With the remaining piece of her board, she rammed it hard into Linus' chest, then ran to grab the chunk.

Her paws held the chip like a piece of gold she would never see again. "Let me the fuck out of here!" she yelled, holding up the chip, and before the goat could protest, she ran to the first door she could find. She ran through the hall, finally finding the stairs down. The demon goat fast behind her, she tumbled through the stairs. She saw his body towering at the top as she stood up, her ankle raging with pain. "Fuck it!" she yelled as she hobbled to the door. She could finally feel it. She could finally feel the air of freedom just waiting past the door she was so eager to enter. Tears started to form at her eyes, a wide smile following, as if the world were a new place and she were ready to enter it. When she touched the doorknob, she looked back, the goat landing at the bottom of the stairs. "Fuck you and fuck your run down house too!" she yelled, leaving through the door and feeling the outside air for the first time in what felt like years.

The moon was bright, brighter than she had imagined when the lioness had first entered the house. A car was driving by and she hobbled to stop it, waving her arm to get its attention. The headlights rolled to a stop. As she narrowed her eyes, Rachel could see a swallow exiting the car. "Holy fuck! Are you okay?!" she screamed, running to Rachel's rescue. Green and grey wings pushed away from her body; she left a trail of feathers as she grabbed the lioness, putting her arm around her. The lioness couldn't say much, her body raging between pain and fear as she was put into the car. As the pair sped off, the lioness looked back at the house. The demon goat stood at the door, eyes following the car as it drove away. He lifted his hand and waved goodbye, his smile still as wide as the moment she first saw it. As the house grew out of sight, Rachel felt her body collapse in her seat. Her eyes were closing, as if to tell her she was safe, that she was going to live.

"What the fuck happened to you?" the swallow asked as she sped her way through the valley of trees and miles rarely seen.

Rachel watched the stars as they drove away, trying to find a way to calm the raging agony her body was feeling. Her breath heavy, air pummeled her lungs as she took in every ounce she could. She didn't know how to respond to the swallow's question, her lips sticking together from being dried out. Her mind flushed with the thought of water; her body craved it, believing she would feel some kind of relief if she just had a drop. Unable to answer, unable to put forth her experience into words, she tilted her head back, watching the sky pass over them. She found Orion battling Scorpius in the sky and she wondered how many ages she would have to battle the goat stuck in her mind. Although she'd escaped, she knew he would be with her always. She knew his smile would pierce her vision when she closed her eyes; she knew her friends' bodies would stay with her; she knew she never really escaped the house.

The swallow put her hand on the lioness' shoulder. Rachel's eyes looked over it, a quiver erupting from her legs. Each time she blinked, she saw his hand, the lithe goat devil's grasp on her shoulder. She knew it wasn't there, but knew it was a grasp that would never leave her. Rachel pushed the bird's hand off of her, and before the swallow could say anything, the lioness felt herself shatter like a hammer to a mirror. Laughter burst from the lioness' mouth; an uncontrollable fit of laughter raged out of her throat as it was all she had left. She mourned by laughing, felt her pain through laughter. Tears streamed down her face as she knew another battle would emerge someday. She just hoped it wouldn't be tomorrow. One day she would have to return. She felt it in her belly. She would have to return to burn the house. How best to deal with horrors left inside of you?

Rachel's head rested against the window of the car, the driver pushing the gas as hard as she could. The laughter made her uncomfortable, but the swallow didn't say anything. She just kept driving. And Rachel just kept laughing.

OTHER TITLES BY THE AUTHOR

Poetry
Born Into This
a warm place to self-destruct
we don't make it out alive
Cut the Loss
We Balanced Gravity as I Ate You Out
Time Passes Like Flames in the Distance
Once More with Noise
The Audacity of Your Bullshit

Fiction
Cigarette Burns
We Live for Half-Moons
Jazz at the End of the Night

Films
Poetry is Dead

CD
a warm place to self-destruct
The Audacity of Your Bullshit

Edited Anthologies
#ohmurr!
Blood, Sweat, and Fists
Body & Blood
Degenerates: Voices for Peace
Difursity
Dread
The Haunted Traveler
Incendiary
Knotted
Ordinary Madness
Passing Through
Purrgatorio
Typewriter Emergencies
Vagabonds: Anthology of the Mad Ones

WEASEL is a Queer, Latinx author and The Dude of Weasel Press. He has appeared in an indie documentary called Something Out of Nothing (S.O.O.N.) directed by Mitchell Dudely, as well as Living art with Dr. Michael Woodson 90.1 KPFT. Weasel is an activist for marginalized voices, a domestic violence survivor, and an author who focuses on queerness, race, and sex positivity. His work has appeared in anthologies such as *Slashers, Infurno, Sinister Sheets, Thirteen Poets, Five2One Magazine, SickLit Mag, Furry Book Review.* In 2016 & 2019 he was a Juried Poet for the Houston Poetry Fest. He currently lives in Michigan with his partner Howl and couldn't be happier.

http://degenerateweasel.weebly.com
Twitter: @systmaticweasel
Twitter (Adult): @systmaticwzl
Instagram: @systmaticwzl

Other Titles from Sinister Stoat Press

The Last Book You'll Ever Read by Scott Hughs
Cause for Concern by Neil S. Reddy
The Devil has a Black Dog by Jonathan W. Thurston
Spiders in our Bed by Jonathan W. Thurston
Body & Blood edited by Weasel
Dread edited by Weasel
Incendiary edited by Weasel
The Haunted Traveler edited by Weasel
Ghostly Pornographers by Thomas White

DARK TITLES FROM WEASEL PRESS & RED FERRET PRESS

POETRY

Pan's Saxophone by Jonel Abellanosa
The Madness of Empty Spaces by David E. Cowen
The Seven Yards of Sorrow by David E. Cowen
Bleeding Saffron by David E. Cowen
Face Down in the Leaves by Dwale
Satan's Sweethearts by Marge Simon and Mary Turzillo
Wolf: An Epic and Other Poems by Z.M. Wise

FICTION

Brinwood by RK Gold
The Goat: Building the Perfect Victim by Bill Kieffer
In and of Blood by Kat Lewis
Taxi Sam in PINK NOIR by Neil S. Reddy
Not Kafka: A Collection of Ugly Shorts by Neil S. Reddy
Tales in Liquid Time by Neil S. Reddy